AF416866

BELLA AND THE SUMMER FLING

A LOVE ON THE TRACK NOVEL

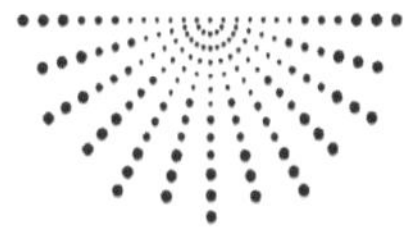

AMY SPARLING

Copyright © 2019 by Amy Sparling

All rights reserved.

No part of this book may be reproduced in any form or by any electronic or mechanical means, including information storage and retrieval systems, without written permission from the author, except for the use of brief quotations in a book review.

BELLA

*I*t's just after midnight. I can hear my brother Brent's phone playing music in the room next to mine. When he lived here full time, he'd always listen to music to fall asleep, and whatever tunes he was obsessed with at the time would soon become my favorite music, too. Now that he's home from college, I guess not everything has changed. He's taller, more muscular, and acts like he's all grown up. But he still needs music to fall asleep.

I finish drying my hair and then I sit on my bed, exhausted from the night, but somehow still unable to sleep. My body feels like every single nerve is awake and ready to party. I'm too excited. Too giddy, too surprised. Too… floaty.

I'm so much of so many feelings right now.

The greatest though, is pride.

I look over at my nightstand, which is now the temporary home of my shiny new trophy. I'll have to find the perfect place to display it tomorrow, but for now, it's right here next to my bed. My smile widens. My new trophy is at least two feet tall, with a white marble stand two sparkly blue columns. At the top, there's a little golden dirt bike with a guy on it. On the bottom, engraved in a small golden plate are the words:

Women's Class
2nd Place

Not bad at all for my first ever race. I may have had a dirt bike since I was six years old, but up until a few weeks ago, I only rode it for fun. I never tried to be particularly fast or talented, because it all seemed too impossible for me to achieve. I just rode around on the dirt bike track, jumping over small jumps, and having fun. It was my hobby, not my career or anything. I didn't need to be fast or spend money on races that I had no chance of winning.

But that all changed when I met Liam Mosely.

He's eighteen like me, but unlike me, he didn't go to high school and waste all his days stuck in a stuffy building with demanding teachers and dramatic classmates. Instead, he's been homeschooled while he focused solely on dirt bike racing, or motocross as it's called professionally. He finally got good enough to race with a professional team last season, but then he was kicked off when he got into not one, but two fist fights with fellow racers. Fighting is unsportsmanlike and against the rules. He was kicked off Team FRZ Frame in a heartbeat, and they didn't care that he had a good reason for doing what he did.

Liam's dad decided to exile him to spend the summer with his mom here in Roca Springs, Texas It's a teensy little country town that no one has ever heard of. And it's where we met. He never did tell me why exactly he got into those fights that derailed his professional career, just that he had a good reason for it. My smile slips a little bit. I don't want to be stupidly crushing on a guy with an anger problem. But the

Liam I know doesn't have one. I believe him when he says he's not normally a fighter.

Tonight I watched him back down from a bet with my brother. He could have gone out there and raced him and totally won because Liam is much faster than Brent. But he didn't. He didn't want to fight, didn't want to cause any more bad blood. So whatever reason made Liam punch those other guys, I'm sure it was justified. Because I hate the idea of crushing on a guy who talks with his fists.

Not that it matters, by the way. I totally can't crush on Liam Mosely.

Even though I just kissed him.

I swear my heart is still beating twice as fast as it should be, even though the night is over. The races are over, and that kiss is over. I came home and ate dinner and showered and now I'm still feeling that dizzying rush of adrenaline and excitement. I guess nights like this will take a while to get over.

I participated in my first ever motocross race and kissed the hottest guy I've ever kissed, all in one night. And now I have a shiny trophy and the memories of Liam's soft lips to remember it by.

This was a good night.

But it can never happen again.

I definitely want to race again, maybe even race several more times. But that kissing Liam thing? Never again. Sure, he's crazy hot and talented and always seems to listen when I'm talking to him, but he's not boyfriend material. Boyfriends don't move back home at the end of summer, and that's exactly what Liam will be doing.

He'll try to get picked back up on another professional race team and I'm sure it'll happen for him. He's too good of a racer to be left out in the cold. He'll get picked up, and he'll race professionally again, and he'll become even more famous and even bigger of a deal than he is now. He'll meet some charming supermodel or maybe even an actress—whoever she is, she'll be gorgeous and perfect—and they'll fall in love and get married and he'll forget all about little ol' me, Bella Castro, the random girl from a small town who kissed him one night after a race.

I take a deep breath and pull down the sheets on my freshly made bed. It's time to go to sleep. Otherwise I'll just sit here and stare at my trophy and think about him all night. I may not be a psychologist, but I know that's not healthy.

I crawl under the covers and lay down, listening to the gentle beat of Brent's music from his bedroom. One full song plays. Then another. Then five more.

Ugh, I can't sleep.

I roll over in bed and grab my phone off the nightstand. My mom hates cell phones because they take away too much of our time. I was one of the last people in school to get my own phone because she hated them so much, but finally when I turned sixteen and started driving, my dad convinced her that I needed one for safety reasons. Mom says you can't enjoy real life when you're looking at a phone all day. I get it, kind of. But my real life happens to be *on* my phone. I check Snapchat and then Instagram, where I scroll through beautiful photos and weird photos and memes until my eyes hurt. It's just after one in the morning. I'm still not tired.

My phone lights up.

Liam: You awake?

Oh crap. He's texting me! In the middle of the freaking night. I should put my phone away. I should turn it off and go to sleep. But…

Me: Yup

My phone rings. It's not just a phone call – Liam Mosely is Facetiming me at one in the morning. *Oh crap. Oh crap, oh crap.* I'm wearing Mickey Mouse pajamas and my hair is in a bun and I have no makeup on! This is not okay!

But maybe that's for the best. If Liam sees me looking like all gross, maybe he'll realize that it's pointless to keep up this flirting thing with me. Maybe he'll stop calling, stop hanging out with me at the track, stop being my friend. Then maybe I can finally get over him and move on with my life.

I sit up in bed and I answer the call.

"You're up pretty late," I say in a voice just above a whisper. Brent is in the next room over, after all and he will flip if he knows I'm talking to Liam.

Liam is wearing a black shirt, and he looks just as heart-crushingly hot as ever. He smirks. "You're one to talk."

I roll my eyes. "I was about to go to sleep."

"Want me to let you go?"

I shake my head. "I can talk. What's up?"

"Why are you whispering?" he says, leaning closer to the phone when he says the last word.

I feel a blush creep to my cheeks. "My brother is in the next room," I say. "It's better if he doesn't wake up."

Liam's expression goes from playful to somber. "I tried to talk to him. Before your race started, just him and me."

"What?" My eyes widen at my outburst and I remind myself to go back to a whisper. "You did? What did you say?"

He shrugs one shoulder, then lays back in his bed. He's holding the phone above him and I can almost imagine that I'm standing in his room looking down at him while he lays in bed. The thought does weird things to my stomach.

"I told him I was sorry," Liam says. "He didn't seem to care."

"Wow." Brent hadn't told me about this. He was excited for my first race and he was happy for me on the whole drive home, but he never mentioned this.

"He just needs time," I say, and for all I know, that's probably a lie. My brother hates Liam. I don't think he'll stop hating him any time soon, unfortunately.

Liam's lips twist into a smile. It's a little forced, like maybe he's trying not to think about my brother's lack of goodwill toward him. "So what did you think of your first race?"

"It was exhilarating. And amazing," I say. I want to lay down, too, but that feels somehow too intimate. So I keep sitting up on my bed, looking at my phone for the video chat. "It was scary, too, but mostly fun. I owe it all to you."

"Nah, you did this. It was all you."

I shake my head. "You gave me the skills and the confidence to race. You have no idea how long I've wanted to get out there and race."

His eyes soften. "I'm glad you had a good time. My first race was a disaster."

"Oh yeah?"

He nods. "I was six years old and I thought I was a little badass." He chuckles at the memory. I had drank a whole bottle of chocolate milk on the drive to the track, and it was the middle of the summer, so it was like a hundred degrees outside. I was so nervous, and it was so hot, and when I was at the starting line, my stomach started hurting. All I had all day was that chocolate milk. No food, no water. And then halfway through the race, it came back up."

He cringes at the memory. "I puked half curdled, hot, chocolate milk while I was riding. It got all over my helmet and my clothes. It was so gross."

"Eww!" I say with a laugh. "That's awful."

"Yeah it was," Liam says with a smile that makes my own stomach hurt. "I didn't even finish the race. My very first race, and I got a DNF."

"I'm sorry," I say.

"Nah, it's all good. I went back the next weekend, and my

dad made sure I didn't have any chocolate milk. I think I got tenth place. I sucked. But I didn't care, I just wanted to keep racing until I won."

"And how long did that take?" I ask.

His teeth bite down on his bottom lip. "Longer than I care to admit."

"Whaaaat?" I say sarcastically. "You mean the great Liam Mosely wasn't always a winner?"

"Not even close." He turns on his side to talk to me. Now it looks like we're laying next to each other… if, well, if I was his phone. I'd be right next to him.

"I think I was around eight or nine before I won a race. It was hard. It took a lot of work, and my dad only brought me to the track. He'd sit on his phone or his laptop the whole time, doing work. He couldn't teach me anything because he didn't ride dirt bikes, and he didn't care about the sport. I think he just kept taking me to the track because he felt bad about the divorce. But I kept riding, and I learned from watching others, and soon I got better."

I yawn. "When did your parents divorce?"

"When I was six."

"Wow, me too," I say. "I hated it. Brent didn't really care much. Or at least he acted like he didn't care. My parents are still friends, though."

"Yeah, mine are too." He shrugs. "Kind of. My mom got remarried, and she's pretty happy now. Phil is a good guy."

"Plus she lives in Roca Springs, so clearly your mom is awesome," I say with a grin.

He rolls his eyes. "I don't know about that. I prefer the big city life."

We keep talking, about our childhood memories, and dirt bikes, and television shows. I don't know when it happens, but soon I'm lying down, too, watching Liam through the phone while he lays in his bed.

We talk about a lot of things. And we don't talk about that kiss we shared tonight. I find myself staring at his lips while he talks, imagining what it would be like to kiss him again. For real this time. Not as a silly bet. Not as a joke.

Another yawn overtakes me.

"I should let you get to sleep," Liam says, his voice soft and soothing. He's nothing like the arrogant version of himself that's often portrayed on YouTube or articles from motocross magazines. He's sweeter in real life.

"I don't want to go to sleep," I say, just as my stupid mouth betrays me and breaks into a yawn again.

He laughs. "It's almost three in the morning."

"Really?" I say, glancing at the time. "Wow."

"Go to bed," Liam says, peering softly into the phone. He looks so cute right now, his hair all messy on his pillow. "We'll talk tomorrow."

I nod as I yawn again. "Okay. Goodnight."

I hang up and drop my phone on the nightstand. Then I sink into my pillow and close my eyes. My whole body feels warm, electrified. I'm really not supposed to have a crush on Liam Mosely.

But right now, I don't really care.

2

LIAM

I wake up to the sound of not-so-quiet whispers just outside my bedroom. It's been a few weeks but it's still hard getting used to living in a house full of people. At home in Houston, it's just my dad and me and he never makes any sound, mostly because he's never home.

"You ask him!"

"No, *you* ask him!"

"I don't think he's awake yet!"

I blink a few times and sit up in the twin bed that's my temporary home here in Roca Springs. Man, I miss my bed at home. It's a king size memory foam mattress and I never wake up with my body feeling all cramped in such a small place when I'm at home. I don't complain though, because I know my mom is doing the best she can with putting me up for the summer.

The loud whispers are back. "Just knock on the door!"

I chuckle. The voices are from my little step-brothers, Matt and Dylan. They're not twins, and even though they're two years apart, they still look like twins in everything but height. I've only been around them, and my step-father Phil, a few times since my mom married into their family about five years ago. I'm not exactly a big fan of little kids, but Matt and Dylan are okay. They're well behaved and they love my mom. Their mom died from heart failure when they were still infants, so my mom is the only mom they know. She loves them both to death, so I'm going to make it a point to be a good big brother.

"I'm awake," I call out. The whispers stop immediately. "You guys can come in."

A few seconds later, my door slowly opens and Matt and Dylan peer into my room.

It's actually the office and junk room where Mom and Phil store things they don't have a place for, but it's my room for the summer.

"Hi," Matt says. At least, I think it's Matt. They're too similar looking to tell apart sometimes. I think I can tell them apart based on haircuts and height, but I try not to call them by name just in case I get it wrong.

"What's up?" I ask.

They both step nervously into my room, looking at each other like they hope the other one will speak up.

Finally, Matt says, "Dad and Mom are going shopping—"

"They're running errands," Dylan interrupts.

"It's going to take all day," Matt says with a nod.

"And, well, Mom said maybe you could—"

Matt bounces on his toes and words tumble out of his mouth. "Maybe you could take us to the park."

I laugh. The way they were acting, you'd think they were going to ask me to donate a kidney.

"Sure," I say, standing up and stretching. "Where's the park?"

"It's by the grocery store," Dylan says. "It's a huge park and there's ice cream and people bring their dogs and stuff. Sometimes you get to pet the dogs."

His brother nods eagerly. "Dad gave us money for ice cream. I have enough money to get you ice cream too."

Oh, to be a kid and think that a day with ice cream is the best thing to happen to you. Sometimes I wish I could go back in time to when I was that small and carefree. Now I'm saddled with the worry over my professional racing career, the awkwardness of living with my mom for the summer, and the fact that I can't get a certain girl out of my mind even though I'm in no position to be dating.

Speaking of, I definitely need a distraction from worrying about two of those things. The girl thing – well I'm happy to think about her all day.

"Sounds good," I say. "Let me get dressed and then we'll head out.

The boys look at each other, their eyes matching expressions of excitement. "Yay!"

I take a quick shower and get dressed. When I emerge into the living room, my mom and Phil are getting ready to leave. Mom gives me a big bear hug, which is a little weird for her. We haven't been extremely close in our lives, and that's definitely my fault.

"I'm proud of you," she says, squeezing my upper arms as she looks at me. "We're going furniture shopping so we'll be a while. You boys have fun today."

I'm not sure why she's proud of me, but I'll take it. My mom was a little harsh on me when I first got here a month ago. I can't say I blame her. Still, it's nice to be on her good side again. She's a great woman, and I never saw that when I was growing up. All I cared about was dirt bikes, and motocross was a Dad sport, not a Mom one.

Matt and Dylan tug on their shoes in the living room while they talk excitedly about which parts of the park they're going to play on first. Mom and Phil leave after Phil gives me another twenty dollars just in case the boys want more than ice cream. I tell him I don't mind spending my own money, but he insists. Man, this guy is nice.

"Do you guys mind if I invite a friend?" I ask the boys once our parents are gone.

"We don't care," Dylan says.

I pull up Bella's name on my phone. She's the last person I called and texted, so her name is right there beckoning to me to call her. "What's the name of the park?"

"Broken Pines Park," Dylan says.

I call Bella, and I try very hard not to listen to that little voice in my mind that's telling me this might be a bad idea. She's just someone I see at the dirt bike track, and someone I give riding lessons to. We're not supposed to like each other. We're not supposed to date. But a trip to the park to babysit two kids isn't a date, right? If anything, it's a chore. Being surrounded by kids at a park isn't romantic at all.

"Good morning," Bella says, sounding chipper. I wonder if she got a great night's sleep after we finally got off the phone last night. I know I did. I fell asleep quickly and had a dozen dreams, all involving her and that one kiss we shared at the track.

"It's almost noon," I say.

"It's still morning to me. Someone rudely kept me up late last night so I only woke up half an hour ago."

"Wow, he sounds like a great guy," I tease. "You should probably hang out with him today."

"And what did he have in mind?"

"Broken Pines Park?"

"Really?" she says. The tone of her voice is very much indicative of the fact that teenagers, especially those who are legal adults now, don't hang out at parks. Like I said… totally not romantic. So it's no big deal that I'm inviting her, right? We're just friends, doing a friendly thing.

"Yeah… I have babysitting duty today and I promised my

step-brothers I'd take them to the park. I thought maybe you'd want to hang out. There's ice cream in it if you say yes."

"Well, I can't say no to ice cream," she says. "What time are you going? I'll meet you there."

"I can pick you up," I say, reaching for my truck keys off the rack by the garage door. "We're about to leave."

"Nah, I'll just meet you there?"

It feels stupid, but my pride is a little hurt that she doesn't want to ride with me. "Are you sure? It saves gas if we take one car."

She laughs. "That park is right behind my house. I can walk there."

My pride is restored, if only slightly. I laugh, too. "See you soon."

"Is that your girlfriend?" Matt says as soon as I hang up the phone.

"No," I say, holding my keys. "Let's go."

"Then why did you look like she's your girlfriend?" Dylan says.

"I didn't look like anything."

"Yes you did," the boys say in unison.

"You kids want ice cream?" I ask.

"Yes!"

"Then don't mention the word girlfriend again."

I'm trying to be intimidating, but they just snicker and look at each other as if we're sharing some private secret. Kids are the worst.

Broken Pines Park is surprisingly awesome. It reminds me a little bit of the Houston Zoo back at home, and nothing like the small park I imagined it would be. It's huge, and it has several playground areas, all with different themes from outer space to animals to pirates. There are a few manmade lakes with wooden bridges that cross over them, and picnic tables with BBQ pits scattered around. One section of the park is for dogs, and my step-brothers want to visit that part first so they can get their fill of petting every dog in sight.

The main park road is lined with food trucks and little kiosks that sell balloon animals, jump ropes, battery powered fans, and everything a little kid could want. I text Bella and tell her that we're in the dog park section, and she says she's on her way.

My whole body feels stretched thin with anticipation. I talked to her on the phone for hours last night, but it wasn't enough. It's not the same as seeing her in person. Plus, I didn't tell her about Team Loco last night. I don't know why. I kept wanting to mention it, but I didn't. Today, I will tell her.

Matt and Dylan are laying on the ground being attacked with Golden Retriever kisses when I finally see her.

She's wearing black shorts and a white tank top that's all sparkly and looks cute on her. Her light brown hair hangs loose around her shoulders, and even from several feet away, I can tell she's wearing makeup. Her skin looks angelic, and her eyes are sparkly and her lips are pinker than usual. Glossier, too.

Did she get dressed up for me?

Every single time I've seen this girl it has been at the dirt bike track, where everyone is dirty and sweaty and not looking their best. Motocross is a sport, after all, and you get sweaty and dirty when riding. That doesn't matter where Bella is concerned. Even covered in dirt, she's gorgeous.

But this is some next level beauty right now.

"Wow," I say. Like an idiot. I can't believe the word just fell out of my mouth like that. I'm supposed to play it cool.

We're just friends, after all, and friends don't comment on the other one looking absolutely gorgeous.

"Wow, what?" she says.

I have to save face, and fast. "Wow, you got here quick," I say.

She points to the main road, which cuts right between a large suburban neighborhood. "I live right over there."

"Cool," I say.

She smiles up at me.

"You look beautiful."

Crap. Again with my stupid mouth.

Bella blushes and tucks her hair behind her ear. "You look beautiful, too."

"Do I?" I say, glancing down at my khaki shorts and Yamaha T-shirt.

She laughs. "Of course."

My little brothers take this opportunity to come running up to us. We've only been here about fifteen minutes and they already smell like a sweaty boy's locker room.

"Can we get ice cream now?"

"Sure thing," I say. "Bella, this is Matt and Dylan."

"Hi!" the boys say to her, and to my great relief, they don't say anything else. I guess they can be trusted to keep their girlfriend thoughts to themselves after all.

They run ahead toward the ice cream food truck while Bella and I walk behind.

"I forgot you had brothers," she says, her hands shoved in her pockets.

It's a good thing too, otherwise, I might try to hold her hand.

"They're my step-brothers," I say. "I don't know if I've talked about them much"

She kicks an acorn across the road. "I'm not sure you

have. Maybe you mentioned them once, but I always assumed you were an only child."

"My mom lives with her husband, Phil, and his two kids. I didn't really know them well before I moved here," I admit. "We're getting closer now, but they still feel like strangers. Plus Matt and Dylan are so young, I have no idea how to connect with them besides buying them ice cream."

"My best friend has twin little brothers and they're annoying. At least yours are fun to be around."

"Give them time," I say with a laugh. "They know how to get pretty annoying, too."

"Do you have any other siblings?"

I shake my head. "My dad never remarried, and I don't even know if he dates anyone, to be honest. He works a lot and keeps to himself. If he could marry his job, he probably would."

Bella glances up at me while we walk, and the sunlight dances off the sparkles in her lip gloss. I've never wanted to kiss her as badly as I do right now. *Not cool, Liam. Chill out.*

Bella's lips lift into a soft smile. "Isn't it weird how we've spent like every day together this summer and we still don't know much about each other?"

"Speaking of that…"

A look of alarm flashes across her face. I smile to show her that she doesn't have anything to worry about. "I've been wanting to talk to you about something cool that happened."

"Oh yeah?"

We've reached the ice cream truck and my brothers are practically bursting at the seams with their desire for sugary ice cream cones. I tell them they can get whatever they want, and their little kid energy ramps up to intense levels.

They order cones with three scoops and sprinkles and chocolate syrup on top. I'm pretty sure this is going to result in a massive mess at some point, but whatever. They're kids.

I want them to have fun, and hopefully their sticky hands won't ruin the interior of my truck later on.

After looking over the extensive menu that's on the side of the food truck, I order a mint chocolate chip cone.

"Ooh!" Bella says, looking at me with wide eyes that remind me of Matt and Dylan. I guess ice cream brings out the little kid in her. She turns to the guy behind the window. "I'll have the same thing."

"You gonna let me pay for it?" I ask, playfully poking her in the side. She didn't want me to pay for her food at the dirt bike track.

She considers it for a moment. "Sure."

It's just a three dollar ice cream, and it's not a big deal, but it feels like it is. She's letting me buy her something. She's letting me treat her like she's special and not just some girl. This kind of makes it a date. But I keep my thoughts to myself.

The boys get their ice cream monstrosities and run toward a nearby park bench to eat them. I say a silent prayer that none of that chocolate gets all over my truck seats on the drive home.

Bella and I walk to our own park bench across from the boys. I need to keep an eye on them, but I also don't want them hearing all my business. The last thing I need is for them to start asking if she's my girlfriend again.

Bella licks her ice cream cone and I try very hard to stop thinking about kissing her. The feelings I have for her aren't just skin deep. I'm realizing this as I watch her, while she looks absolutely stunning, sitting in the sun right next to me. This isn't like me at all. I'm not the guy who falls for girls. I'm the guy who spends all my time working on my career.

I have to stop feeling this way. I have to stop crushing so very hard on her. Instead of sitting here watching her and thinking about how badly I want to kiss her, I need to change the subject. I say the first thing that comes to mind. "I got an offer from Team Loco."

"What!" Her smile reaches all the way to her eyes and it makes me wish I'd brought this up sooner. "When? Liam! That's amazing!"

"The other day," I say. Her enthusiasm is infectious. Suddenly I wish I had told her about this last night instead of talking about all the pointless things I said to avoid this topic. "It's probationary for one season, but if I get through it with no drama or anything, then I'll be signed on for good."

"Team Loco is pretty popular." Bella turns her cone around, quickly licking up a few wayward drips before they go too far. "I think they're even better than Team FRZ Frame."

"I think so too," I say. Why can't I stop looking at her? Every single thing she does is adorable.

I pull my gaze away and glance at my brothers.

"I'm really excited for you," Bella says. "This is big. You'll be extra famous after next season."

I chuckle. "It's a catch 22, I guess. I want to race professionally, but I'm not exactly happy about the fame that follows."

"Well don't forget about us small town people when you make it big."

I look back at her, and she's watching me with the cutest expression. She's waiting for something. I'm not sure what, but I know it's the same thing I'm waiting for too.

Oh, screw it.

"I'll never forget you," I say. Then I lean over and kiss her as if we are electric and we need each other to survive. As if we're magnetic and if I don't make it very quick, we'll get stuck together and I'll never stop kissing her.

Not that an eternity of kissing Bella would be a bad thing...

When I pull away, she looks surprised, but in a good way.

"You taste like mint chocolate chip," she says, staring right into my eyes. Right into my freaking soul.

"So do you."

Oh man, I never want this summer to end.

3

BELLA

*J*lick my ice cream cone so I have an excuse to look away from Liam. If it were up to me, I'd stare at the boy every second of every day. He's just that gorgeous. He's all toned muscles and crisp haircuts and cocky smirks that drive me insane.

I knew it the moment I first saw him at the bike shop, when he rudely cut in front of me in the checkout line. He's since told me he didn't realize he was cutting that day, and I believe him. But yeah, even back then, I knew he was hot. The type of hot that transcends regular guys in high school. He's got soft dirty blond hair that's just long enough to run my fingers through (not that I ever have, but man, I want to), and that sharp jawline that matches his streamlined muscles. I've seen him without his shirt on several times at the dirt bike track, and every time it's hard not to stare. The boy is gorgeous.

A lot of professional motocross racers are attractive, but Liam Mosely is at the top of that list.

I can't believe he got offered a sponsorship on Team

Loco. Well… I guess I can believe it. He's a great rider and he's extremely fast. I guess the part I can't believe is that he's moving on, and I'm still stuck here.

While we sit here on this park bench eating our ice cream cones, I tell him I am so proud of him and so happy and that I can't wait to see him wearing the Team Loco colors in the fall racing season. He tells me about the phone call he got and how the manager seemed like a cool guy who really had faith in him.

It's extremely cool, and I'm so happy for him. But the more we talk about his future, the more I realize I don't have a future lined up for myself. Sure, the days will come and go, and summer will soon be over. It's inevitable. But what I am I going to do after that?

Now that high school is over, I feel so incredibly lost. I've never been someone who knew what I wanted to do as a career, unlike my best friend, Kylie, who has wanted to be a high school teacher for as long as I can remember. She wants to teach English or theater arts and she's already registered for Texas State University, just like most high school seniors did this year. Everyone I know already had their college plans in place before we graduated.

I'm the lone straggler with no idea what to do. I'm that person the posters on the walls of guidance counselors everywhere warn you not to be.

"You okay?" Liam nudges me softly with his elbow. His ice cream is nearly gone, but I still have half of mine left. The boy eats everything much faster than I do. Maybe it helps that he's not sitting here contemplating his boring future like I am.

"I'm just thinking about life," I say.

He chuckles. "That's a little generic. Anything specific?"

I look him in his hazel eyes and it feels like I can tell him anything. It doesn't matter that he's leaving after summer. It doesn't matter that we're not exactly dating, but we're not exactly just friends either. He feels solid, like a rock that's planted in the middle of a river. Like someone I can trust just as much as I want to kiss.

I press my lips together, trying to ignore all thoughts of kissing, and then release my secret thoughts. "High school is over and I have no idea what I'm going to do with my life."

"Hmm," Liam says. He pops the last bite of his ice cream cone in his mouth. "That might be beyond my scope of advice-giving."

I laugh. "I know, right? All my friends are going to college or trade school, and I have no idea what I'm going to do."

"What do you want to do?" he asks.

I shrug. "I literally have no idea. I don't want to be a teacher. I don't want to wear suits and work in fancy corporate buildings like my brother. I also don't want to work some crappy minimum wage job, so I need an education. I just don't know what."

"I've always wanted to race motocross," Liam says, glancing at his brothers who finished with their ice cream on the bench across from us. He leans back on the bench and stretches his arms out. "But you need a backup plan for that kind of career. If I get injured and can't ride anymore or something like that—I'd need something to fall back on."

"So what's your plan B?" I ask.

He looks up as his little brothers run to a swing set to play. We can easily see them from here, so he leans back and looks at me, his arm still slung casually across the back of the bench. I desperately want to lean back too, and cuddle up in his arms. It would be so easy. But that would be weird. We can only be friends, and this isn't a real date, I tell myself.

"Online college classes," he says. "I can get an entire

general studies bachelor degree online from the state university."

"Wow," I say, as the gears turn in my own mind. Maybe I could do the same thing. "I didn't know that."

He nods. "I'm signed up for a full-time course load this fall, and hopefully I can manage that plus racing. The races are only one day a week, and we travel and train a lot, but I think it'll be fine since I can study on the plane and in the hotels. I don't have the time to go to real college with racing, but online classes will be just like when I was homeschooled in high school. That way, even if something happens to derail my professional career—God I hope not—I'll still have a bachelor degree to fall back on."

"Wow," I say, leaning forward and resting my elbows on my knees. "Everyone has a plan but me. You have two plans. I've got nothing."

His hand is warm on my back. "Don't stress, Bella."

I look back at him, and nausea rises up in my stomach. It's easy for him to tell me not to stress... he doesn't have anything to stress about! I feel sick and panicky and I'm not entirely sure why. I think it's fifty percent because I have no idea what to do with my future and fifty percent because Liam's arm is around me and I love the feeling of it so much that it hurts. Summer will be over soon and he won't be here anymore. He won't be here to put his arm around me. He won't be here to kiss me. He won't buy me ice cream. He'll be traveling the country and taking college classes and making a life for himself while I'm stuck here living in my mom's house with no idea what to do.

"Whoa," Liam says, sitting up. "Bella? You look like you've seen a ghost."

I stand up and wring out my hands, trying to quell my anxiety. "Don't worry about me," I say, pacing a few steps away before turning around and then doing it all over again. "I'm just freaking out."

Liam frowns, then stands and moves in front of me, stopping me in my tracks. "Bella, come here." He holds out his arms and I don't even think twice about walking into them. He wraps me in his strong embrace, and I let my face press against his chest. His chin rests on top of my head and for thirty whole seconds, the world feels perfect. My heart slows from its panicked state and soon the smell of cedar and all this fresh air and Liam's cologne starts to make me feel better.

I slowly pull away. "Thanks," I mumble.

"You're only eighteen," Liam says, letting his fingers trail down my arms as he slowly releases me. "You have time to figure out your life. I promise. I'll help you, too. We can go through every career in the world and see which one you like the best."

I grin. "Will there be ice cream involved?"

His smirk is so adorable it makes my toes tingle. "Always."

WE SPEND HOURS AT THE PARK, AND IT'S THE MOST FUN I think I've ever had here. Broken Pines Park has evolved a lot since I was a little kid and would come here with my parents and Brent. There are food vendors and games and more things to do. Liam lets his little brothers get their face painted, and they both pick Captain America shields on their cheeks, which I soon find out is Liam's favorite superhero. The boys look up to Liam and try to copy everything he does. He's a good big brother even if he's not very experienced at it.

We walk around and play on the various playgrounds, and after my slight breakdown over what I'm going to do with my life, we don't talk about any more important subjects. We just have fun.

Liam gets a call from his mom, and then has to break the news to his brothers. "Sorry guys, dinner is almost ready. It's time to go home."

I expect the boys to beg and plead to stay longer, but they handle the news better than I did when I was a kid. They don't even complain.

"So, uh," Liam says, turning to me as we walk back to where his truck is parked. "My mom invited you over for dinner."

My eyes widen. "What?"

He shrugs. "They're just ordering a bunch of pizza, so it's not a big deal." His tongue flicks over his bottom lip and he reaches out his hand, one finger looping around mine. "You should come."

I know it's a bad idea but… "Okay."

He grins and opens the passenger door of his truck for me. "Kiddos in the back," he says.

On the short drive back, we jam out to the radio and sing along to an old rock song. I can't believe the boys know the words, but they do and they belt them out louder than Liam and me. It's not until we pull into the driveway of a cute suburban two-story home that I realize I'm about to meet Liam's mom and step-dad. Holy crap. *I'm meeting his mom and step-dad!*

I draw in a deep breath. I remind myself, for the thousandth time, that we're just friends. It's not like I'm Liam's girlfriend, so there won't be any pressure placed on me with first impressions. So who cares? This is No. Big. Deal.

The back doors open and the boys go tumbling out, running at full speed to the front door. It seems like everything those kids do is always done at full speed.

Liam's hand closes over mine. "They're really nice people. You have nothing to worry about."

"How'd you know?" I ask.

He winks. "I'm a mind reader. And your thoughts are written all over your face."

I bite my lip and I can't say I disagree. My face is probably the picture perfect example of "freaked out" right now.

As soon as we walk inside, my nerves are at an all-time high. A short woman with long dirty blonde hair pops out of the kitchen and smiles at me.

"Hi, sweetheart," she says, hugging me in that Southern Hospitality way that comes naturally to a lot of Texas mons. "You must be Bella. I'm Ruby."

"It's nice to meet you," I say. I'm not about to call her by her first name, because my southern parents taught be better than that, but I realize I have no idea what her last name is. It's probably not Mosely since she divorced Liam's dad and remarried. Oh crap. I guess I can't call her anything until I find out.

"We're out of napkins, so this will have to do." A tall, lanky man in his early forties walks out from the kitchen, holding a roll of paper towels. "Oh, hi there," he says when he notices me. "Are you the famous Bella?"

I look at Liam. "I'm famous?"

If he wasn't so confident and cocky looking all of the time, I'd swear he might be a little embarrassed right now. "I told them about your first motocross race," he says. "And how I helped you train for it."

"Second place on her first try!" his mom says. "That's pretty impressive."

I thank her and hope I don't sound as awkward as I feel. His family is nice. So nice that I desperately want them to like me, even though it doesn't matter one bit because soon summer will be over and Liam will be gone and I'll probably never see them again.

"Dinner is in the kitchen," Liam's step-dad says. "We went a little crazy ordering pizza, so there's several types to choose from. We have soda, tea, and water, too. Help yourself."

"Sounds great, thank you."

Liam turns to me. "Before I forget, let me show you that college site I told you about."

I have no idea what he's referring to, but I follow him out of the living room and down the hall to a bedroom. He opens the door, urges me inside quickly, and then presses it closed behind us. It looks like we're in an office, or maybe a room that hasn't been fully unpacked yet. There's a desk with a computer and filing cabinets, and plastic storage bins all along one side. A small bed is pressed against the wall on the other side, a large suitcase open and piled with clothes next to it.

"What college site?" I say.

"There is no college site," he says. His teeth press into his bottom lip. "I'm sorry, but you look so beautiful, and I had to get us away from my family for just a second could I could do this."

He closes the distance between us in two strides and soon his hands are on my cheeks, tilting my face up to meet his. "Is this okay?" he whispers.

My answer is a soft, "Yes."

He kisses me. Our lips crush together eagerly, impatiently. My heart jackhammers its way across my chest but I lean closer, slide my arms up to his shoulders, and let the kiss go places I've only been imagining. I feel his hands slide down my back, leaving a trail of tingles in their wake. I am out of breath, but I don't care. His lips are the medicine that keeps my heart beating. I don't ever want to break away.

But eventually, we pull back. It's only been a few seconds, and it definitely hasn't been long enough, but time is not on our side. Not now, while pizza and family wait in the other room, and not ever.

I realize, for yet another time, that in just a few weeks the summer will be gone.

And so will Liam.

4

LIAM

It's ironic how I used to wake up in this small bed in the guest bedroom of my mom's new house and hate everything about it. Each day I woke up here was a reminder that I wasn't home in Houston, that I had been kicked off Team FRZ Frame, and that I was stuck living in this small pointless town for the summer. For several days in a row, I would wake up, remember where I am, and get really frustrated.

Funny how things change.

The bed is still uncomfortable, and it's still a little jarring to wake up in a room that's not mine, but now I wake up happy for the day to come, especially if it's a day I'm going riding at the local motocross track.

I load my dirt bike into the bed of my truck and I give Bella a call. "I'm heading to the track. What about you?"

"Same," she says.

"Do you want me to come pick you up?" I wish I didn't sound so pathetically eager, but it is what it is. "That way you don't have to load your bike."

"No… I'll just meet you there."

"You sure?" I grab my gear bag and toss it in the back of my truck. "It's better for the environment if we ride together."

"That might be true, but it's better for the world if we wait to do that kind of thing until Brent leaves. He's taking a six-week summer course at the college but it doesn't start until next week."

"Ah," I say. "Gotcha."

Bella's older brother hates me with a capital H. Doesn't matter that I've apologized to him a few times. Doesn't matter that Bella has begged him to give me a chance. He's not budging on his hatred. It's all because when I was very stupid, I kissed his ex-girlfriend. It didn't mean anything to me, and she was totally the one playing him, but it doesn't matter. He hates me. End of story.

I drive to the track alone and unload my bike. Roca Springs Motocross Park isn't too shabby. It's smaller than the big tracks but the owner really cares about it, so he keeps the track in great shape. People think it's just a pile of dirt, but it's more than that. The jumps have to be releveled and flattened every few days so they stay safe. The track has to be watered down with the large water truck once a day or it'll get too dusty and hardpacked, making riding a nightmare. Maintaining a motocross track is a full-time job. What this track lacks in pomp and circumstance, they make up for by having a solid track.

Not long after I arrive, Bella drives up in her old black Chevy truck. The thing has seen some better days, but she loves it. She parks next to me at our favorite spot, which is off to the side of the track under an old oak tree. No one bothers us over here, not even my overly fanatic fans.

She walks up to me, all smiles.

"The track looks great today." Before I can say anything

else, Bella throws her arms around my neck and presses her lips to mine.

Whoa.

I kiss her back – I would be stupid not to – but then I pull back a bit.

"What's this for?"

She shrugs. "I wanted to do it."

I grin. "Want to do it a second time?"

Her gaze turns sultry as she leans up and kisses me again. I breathe her in, trying to fill my heart and my mind with every inch of this experience so I can relive it later.

She doesn't pull away after a few seconds. Instead, she slides her fingers up my neck, tangling them in my hair. Our mouths part and I deepen the kiss, slowly at first. But my unrestrained passion is getting hard to control and soon we're full on making out in the space between our trucks.

Bella flinches and steps away. She runs a hand over her mouth and looks around. "We can't do this."

My heart deflates. "Okay," I say. "Sorry."

"No." She shakes her head. "Don't be sorry—it's not your fault, it's just—" She exhales slowly and looks up at me. "This is going to hurt like hell."

"I know," I say.

"You're leaving after summer."

"I know."

"And we'll be done."

I nod.

She runs a hand through her hair and shifts on her feet. "And that's the funny thing," she says after a moment of thought. "I don't think I care."

"What do you mean?" I say.

Her bottom lip rolls under her teeth while she thinks. "I like you, Liam. I know it's pointless. I know you're leaving and you're going to be famous and I'm going to be stuck here in this small town forever. But… whatever this is.. I like it."

"*This* …is a lie," I say. "It's fun, don't get me wrong, but it's a lie."

"What if it's just for the summer?"

I stare at her, perplexed and amazed and scared all at once. "Like a fling?"

She shrugs one shoulder. "If you want to label it."

"You're suggesting we have a summer fling?" I say again.

"No strings attached," she says with a nod. "We can keep doing this kissing thing and hanging out every day, and after summer, it'll just be over."

"I don't know, Bella." I can't believe I'm saying this, but it has to be said. I lick my lips and draw on my courage. "It sounds fun, but it also sounds hard. I don't want to let you go after summer."

She rolls her eyes. "What, you want to date me?"

Yes, I think. But she scoffs sarcastically and says, "Obviously not. This can't happen. We're too different and our lives aren't compatible. But for the summer, it could be fun. Just only for the summer."

She steps closer to me, and reaches out, touching my arm. Her soft fingers slide down to my hand, where she holds it lightly. "What do you say?"

"I can't tell you no," I say. I don't even realize I'm leaning closer to her until my hand is on her waist. I press my forehead to hers. "I want whatever you want."

"I want a summer fling," she says, grinning up at me like this is a fun game and not a potential heartbreaking big mistake. "I want to know what it's like to be your girl, if only for a few weeks."

I chuckle. "I haven't dated in a while. I might be bad at it."

"Just keep doing what you're doing," she says, wrapping her arms around me.

I kiss her on the top of her head. I'm not sure why, it just comes naturally. She always smells like coconuts and vanilla, and exactly like the best part of summer.

"Are you sure you're okay with this?" I ask. I almost feel like I need her to answer the question a hundred times before I'll believe it.

"I'm good," she says, peering up at me. "We're eighteen. I think it would be violating a major rite of passage if we skipped having a summer fling. It's all the rage, I've been told."

She grins, and I can't help but smile back.

"Okay then," I say. I know this is going to hurt, but I don't care. Bella knows this will hurt, but she doesn't care.

I take her hand in both of mine and look deep into her eyes. "Want to be my summer fling?"

She laughs and the sound is music to my ears. "Yes I do."

5

BELLA

The good news is that it's only been three days. But the bad news is that it's already been three days. My summer with Liam is growing shower by the day, hour, minute. Every time I think about it, more time has passed and I'm sure that before long, summer will be over and he'll be gone. I try to tell myself to live in the moment and to stop freaking out about the future, but that is much easier said than done. I'm having way too much fun to just give it all up in a few weeks.

If I had my way, Liam and I would hang out every second of the day until I got sick of him and wanted him to leave. But as this is real life, that doesn't happen, both because I'm not sure I *can* get sick of him, and because I still have real life things to do. Right now I'm hanging out with my best friend Kylie, who just had me dye her roots back to black. Her natural hair color is a medium brown but for the last year she's been dying it jet black. The color suits her. It makes her look invincible, and maybe that's where she gets all her confidence to flirt with guys.

We're supposed to get lunch soon and then she has to

babysit her brothers this evening. It sucks for her, but it's good for me that my best friend will be busy this evening, because today is race day at the local track. The summer races are always held in the evening when it's cooler outside. Right now it's over a hundred degrees of scorching Texas heat outside. In the winter, you can have a race during the day but in the summer, that would be a deathwish.

This will be my second time racing, and although Kylie really wants to see me race, I'm glad she can't make it tonight. If she came to the track with me then I'd have to treat Liam like he's just a friend. That's the thing with summer flings—it's better if they're a secret. At least, that's what I've decided because I am absolutely not telling anyone about my fling, not even my best friend.

Kylie turns off my hair dryer and gives me a look. She's been sitting at my makeup table blow drying her hair for the last ten minutes. I'm sitting on my bed playing on my laptop. I look up at her. "What?"

Her eyes narrow. "You're hiding something."

"I'm not hiding anything." Dang. My voice was entirely too defensive. Kylie's eyes widen like she heard it, too.

"You're being weird. You're over there smiling to yourself, and that's just weird," she says, turning back to look at her reflection in the mirror. She brushes out her hair with her fingers. "What are you hiding? Is it a boy?"

"I wish," I say with a snort. It's a complete lie, but I think I pull it off convincingly because she just turns the hair dryer back on.

"You better tell me if you meet a boy."

"You'll be the first to know." It's another lie and I feel terrible about it. Kylie is my best friend in the entire world. Why am I lying to her? I guess I just don't want the drama with Liam to spread any further. We agreed to a fun, no strings attached summer fling. No one needs to know about it. If Kylie knew then she'd warn me about getting my heart broken, or blah, blah, blah. That's why she can't know.

Besides, I've already started the lie. I can't back out now. This thing with Liam will only last a few glorious weeks. And then my life will go back to normal. Kylie will never need to know a thing.

AT THE RACES, LIAM IS ALREADY THERE, PARKED IN OUR SPOT. I've noticed that when we park way out here away from the main parking area, his fans tend to stay away. Whenever he wanders over to the concession stand or the bleachers though, then it's game over and the fans swarm him like he's made of honey. Now that word has gotten out about Liam being offered a position on Team Loco, his fans are even more excited to meet him. I think everyone knows what I know—that Liam will become the next big thing in professional motocross. Everyone wants to say that they knew him before he got big. I'm the opposite. I prefer to think of him as the Liam I know now. Not the future famous athlete.

There are only thirteen races tonight, so the night will end early. That sucks. Most people are happy to have the races over before midnight but this just means less time I get to spend with Liam. If it were up to me, the races would be a two day event. I know, I know. I'm pathetic.

But my whole world feels different around Liam. He sees me. He gets me. He listens when I talk. Unlike the guys I went to high school with, Liam has actual boyfriend potential. Too bad he's a summer fling.

Liam unloads my dirt bike from the back of my truck while I get dressed in my race gear. I'm race number nine tonight, and he's thirteen. The pro class always races last. It's like the big exciting race of the night so they make people wait to watch it.

"Morgan's not here tonight, so you could totally win," Liam says. The way he walks around with this riding pants slung low on his hips, his shirtless torso catching the last rays of sunlight from the day, really makes me short of breath. He's gorgeous, and he knows it.

"She's not?" I say, glancing around. It's not like I could see her though—we're parked pretty far away from everyone else. "What about Maggie?"

"Haven't seen her either," Liam says. "There's a big race at Three Palms this weekend so I think that's where most people are tonight. You've got a real chance of winning."

"Awesome," I say, as I unpack my helmet and boots from my gear bag. "It's too bad Kylie can't come watch me win."

"Why can't she?" he asks.

"She's babysitting."

"She can't just bring her brothers?"

Crap. I don't want to lie to him, too.

I sit on the tailgate of my truck and tug on my socks and boots. "Well… I didn't exactly… invite her," I say, looking down at my boots as I connect all three straps.

"Why not?" Liam asks.

I look at him, hoping the answer will just magically form in his mind. But of course it doesn't. He's going to make me say it, in all of its awkwardness.

"Because she doesn't know about our…arrangement…" I pull on my other boot, focusing on the task instead of looking at him. "And if she came to the race then I'd have to ignore you and act like we're just friends, and that would suck, so it's just better if she's not here."

"You didn't tell her we're just dating for the summer?"

"Dating for the summer." I snort. "That sounds a lot better than summer fling."

"They're the same thing," Liam says.

I shake my head. "But we're not dating. We don't go on dates. We just hang out at the track and stay up all night on the phone."

"We can go on dates," he says.

I give him a look.

"Let's do it." He taps the side of my truck. "Date night. Tomorrow. I'll pick somewhere romantic."

My heart flutters, but instead of showing what I'm feeling inside, I decide to be sarcastic instead. "Are summer flings supposed to be romantic?"

He shrugs on shoulder. "It's *our* summer fling. We get to make the rules."

"I guess I can't argue with that."

The way he smiles at me makes the fluttering in my stomach ramp up into overdrive. "Good," he says, leaning forward and kissing me. "Because summer flings don't have arguments. They just have fun."

I put my hand on his sculpted chest and push him back. "You can't kiss me," I say, feeling a blush creep to my cheeks. "You'll just make me all flustered and then I won't be able to race.

"Got it. Save the kissing for intermission," he says, giving me a wink that makes me melt just as badly as if he had kissed me.

When my race comes up, I'm feeling less nervous than last time. It might be because I've done this before, and because the two fastest women racers in the area aren't here tonight, so there's less competition. I ride up to the starting gate and take my place on the line. When the race begins, I'm actually the first person out of the gate, and it's so exciting to be in front that I'm inspired to keep racing hard. Before I know it, the checkered flag waves and I've just had my first victory.

I see Liam standing near the bleachers. His face is all lit up with excitement and I roll my bike to a stop in front of him and then eagerly pull off my helmet.

"Oh my God!" I say excitedly, because it's all my brain can think of right now.

"You are amazing," he says, taking my helmet from my hands. "First place. You are my best student."

"I am your only student," I say with a laugh.

I'm still sitting on my dirt bike, balancing myself with my toes on the ground. He leans forward until his forehead touches mine. "I wish I could kiss you," he says.

"Too many witnesses," I say back.

He hands me my helmet. "Maybe after I go win my race, we can meet up in my truck for a minute."

Meeting up in his truck is code for making out in his truck. I grin as I slide my helmet back on. "Better hope you win that race."

I ride back to my truck and set my bike on the stand while Liam gets dressed and ready to go out for his race. One thing all the motocross girlfriends do is ride on the back of their boyfriend's bikes up to the starting line where they'll get to watch the race from the best spot on the track. Liam and I can't do that. It would look too obvious, and raise too many questions. So instead, he rides to the starting line alone and I walk up to the bleachers to watch the race with everyone else.

While he's waiting for his race to begin, my phone gets a next text message. It's from my brother.

My heart stops.

The text says: *you want to explain this?*

The image is a screenshot from someone's twitter feed. It has a picture of Liam and me, taken just moments ago when he put his forehead to mine after the race. We're both smiling. We look happy. In love. We look like we're way more than just friends.

Looks like #LiamMosely has himself a Roca Springs girlfriend! the caption says.

I think I'm going to be sick.

6

LIAM

I wake up cold. Freezing cold. I grab the ancient handmade quilt on my small guest room bed and I tug it over myself. It doesn't work. I'm freezing.

I listen for the sound of the air conditioner, but it's not on. I'm just so cold. And… sweaty?

What's going on?

I check the time on my phone and it's six in the morning. The first rays of sunlight filter in through the curtains. I think it's Monday, judging by the sound of Phil and my mom talking in the kitchen. They don't wake up this early on the weekend. Why can't I remember what I did this weekend?

I sit up in bed, shivering from the cold. The moment my feet touch the hardwood floor, I recoil. It's too cold. Everything is too freaking cold.

My head spins and my stomach hurts, but I manage to slide my bare feet into my shoes. I walk out into the house, knowing I look stupid wearing only boxers and shoes.

Mom and Phil look up at me. "Why is it so cold in here?" I ask.

It's summer. It's Texas. It's supposed to be scorching hot

outside and slightly less hot inside as the air conditioning works overtime to cool the place down.

Mom frowns. She gets up and places the back of her hand to my forehead, then just as quickly as she touches me, her hand yanks back. "Liam, you're burning up!"

I blink. "I have a fever?"

"I'll say," she says sarcastically. She pulls open a kitchen drawer and grabs a device that she swipes over my forehead. It beeps and she turns the digital screen toward me. "A fever of a hundred and one. Go back to bed. I'll bring you some Tylenol."

"I can't remember the last time I was sick."

Mom chuckles. "It'll be okay. Just get some rest and lots of fluid. And stay in your bedroom. I don't want the boys to get sick."

As if on cue, Matt walks into the kitchen. "You look gross," he says to me.

"Liam is sick," Mom says. "You boys need to stay away from him so you don't get sick too."

Matt's bottom lip juts out in sympathy as he looks at me. "Did you throw up?"

"Not yet," I say, curling my lip. "I hope I don't, either."

"Hold on!" Matt says. He runs back to his bedroom and then returns, holding a blue stuffed dragon.

"Don't get too close!" Mom says, holding out her hand. "I don't want you boys to get sick."

He tosses the dragon to me. "This will make you feel better."

I smile. "Thanks, kid."

Mom shuttles me back to my room, closing the door behind me to keep out my germs. She brings me water and Tylenol and debates if she should send the boys to their grandmother's house for the week so they don't get sick. While she's doting on me and worrying about the kids, I suddenly remember back when I was a little kid. My mom has always been so caring and loving in times like these. When I lived with Dad, if I got sick he'd hire a babysitter to stay home with me while he worked. The babysitters always did the bare minimum, often forgetting my medicine schedule, and preferring to play on their phones all day.

I've always been left to my own devices when I'm sick. It feels nice to have my mom caring for me now, even though, at eighteen years old, I'm probably too old to be cared for.

I lay back down in bed and warm up with the three extra blankets Mom gives me. Once the medicine kicks in, I feel slightly better. My head isn't so fuzzy and I can think. All I'm thinking about is Bella, but that's not because of my fever. All I ever think about is Bella.

After Friday night's race, I didn't get to see her this weekend because her brother was in town and they were doing family things. I spent the time at home with my brothers, and we went to the mall yesterday, but that's it. I wonder how I got sick. Probably from eating questionable food samples at the food court. The mall is not exactly my idea of fun, but without Bella, I had to find some way to occupy my time.

Now her brother has gone back to college, and we're supposed to meet up at the track today.

I send her a text so she knows I'm not coming.

Me: *bad news. I woke up sick. Like, feeling like death, 101 fever type sick. I can't go to the track today*

Bella: *Oh no! I hope you feel better soon!*

Me: *Thanks. If I stop texting it's because I passed out.*

She doesn't reply right away, and I figure it's for the best if I try to get some rest anyway. It kills me that I don't get to see her, but I'm feeling so incredibly sick, I don't think I could do anything today. My head is in agony, my joints are hurting, and my stomach feels both hungry and in pain at the same time.

I set my phone down and drift off to sleep. When I wake up, my mom is softly calling my name.

"You awake, sweetie?"

Sweetie? That's a new one. I open my eyes and glance toward the door. Mom's standing there, a soft smile on her lips. "You have company."

"Huh?" I sit up in bed and it makes my head spin.

Mom opens the bedroom door all the way and steps aside. Bella walks into my room.

My heart races at the sight of her—all silky long brown hair and sparkly lips and gorgeous eyes. The girl is cute as hell on the dirt bike track, but she's even cuter wearing black leggings and a T-shirt.

"Hi," she says, giving me a bright smile. "I brought you some soup."

"She brought you soup, isn't that sweet?" Mom says. With the sight of Bella in my room, I had forgotten that my mom was even in here. I look over at her, and I'm grateful that I look pale and clammy because otherwise I'd be blushing.

"That is sweet," I say, hoping my mom leaves soon. This is awkward.

"Bella, sweetheart, let me know if you need anything," Mom tells her. "We have drinks in the fridge, so help your-self." Then she flashes my summer fling girlfriend her warm-est, sweetest, Mom Smile before she leaves, closing the door behind her.

"Your mom is nice," Bella says. She's holding a thermal lunch kit in her hands, and a backpack is slung over her shoulders.

"That was a little nicer than usual," I say skeptically. "My mom must really like you."

Bella smiles and sits on the end of my bed. I reach over

and grab a clean shirt from the laundry basket next to my bed and tug it on. I'm still in my boxers underneath all the blankets, and it feels a little awkward, like I'm being too forward with her, even though she can't see my boxers.

"You don't have to get dressed or anything," Bella says, seeing my hesitation. "You relax. I brought you my grandma's famous chicken and dumplings."

She reaches into the lunch kit and removes a steaming hot plastic bowl with a lid. She hands it to me, along with a spoon.

I take a bite. "Did you make this?"

She nods.

I take another bite. "It's really good."

This makes her grin. "So when did you get sick?" she asks.

I tell her about how I felt when I woke up this morning and how it came on suddenly and I'm suspecting the mall was the culprit.

"Ew, yeah," she says, sliding back on the foot of my bed until her back rests against the wall. "The mall is gross."

"Lesson learned," I say. "Sorry my room is so boring."

"No worries," she says. She grabs her backpack off the floor. "I brought us entertainment." She takes out her laptop and positions it on the bed so that we can both see it. We watch Netflix while I eat my chicken and dumplings.

When I'm done, she takes the bowl and spoon and goes to the kitchen to rinse it out. She returns with a fresh bottle of water and two pills in her hand. "Your mom said it's time for another dose," she says, handing it to me.

"You don't have to do all of this," I say as I swallow the pills and lay back on my bed. I've propped up all my pillows so that I'm resting in an inclined position. I wish Bella could snuggle up next to me, but it's better that she sits at the foot of the bed so she won't get sick.

"I don't mind," she says. "That's what summer flings do for each other."

I smile at her and she blushes, then bashfully turns her attention toward the computer screen.

I know she's trying to play it cool, this whole summer fling thing, but it feels like we're more than that. This girl has no obligation to me at all because she's not my real girlfriend. Yet she made me soup and came over to hang out with my sick, gross self. She made me food. She brings me water.

She's caring for me even though I can't do anything for her right now. I am suddenly hit with the realization that this is what I've missed out on all my life. This is what having a real girlfriend would feel like. It's not just holding hands and making out and texting each other every day. A relationship is about caring for the other person even when they're sick and stuck in bed. That's real. That's…

I exhale and look away. This kind of thing isn't okay to think about, or joke about, or even imagine. I can't be tossing around that word in my mind.

She's my summer fling and that's all.

I can't believe I almost thought the word *love*.

7

BELLA

On Wednesday, Liam kicks me out. He does it in the cutest way, though. I came over in the morning and brought him some more chicken and dumplings. He's had them every day this week and he loves them so much that I keep making more.

But as soon as I arrived this morning and gave him his food, Kylie called. I silenced her call and sat down on the foot of Liam's bed.

"How you feeling?"

"About twenty-two percent better," Liam said. "Who was calling?"

I rolled my eyes. "It's just Kylie. She wants to go to the mall. I told her that's a good way to get sick," I said with a laugh.

Liam dove into the food. "I could eat this every day for the rest of my life," he said.

My phone rang again. I glanced at the screen to make sure it wasn't my mom or something, but it was just Kylie.

"You should go with her," Liam said.

I frowned. "But you're sick."

He grinned and ate some more chicken and dumplings. "That's why you should go. You'll just be bored here, and besides… you don't want to be like Kylie."

"What do you mean?" I asked.

"She ditches you when she has a boyfriend. You're a better friend than that."

"You're right," I said, feeling the slightest bit embarrassed. He *was* right. Very right. I've barely seen her all summer because I've been with Liam.

I stood up and patted his leg from on top of his blanket. "You doing okay?"

"I have my chicken and dumplings, so I'm perfect," he said with a cocky grin. Even when he's all feverish and looks like death, he's still the cutest guy ever.

"Call me if you need me," I said.

He grinned. "Don't worry, I will."

I KNOW I MADE THE RIGHT CHOICE IN SEEING KYLIE TODAY. She seems extra happy to hang out, and besides, Liam is just my fake summer fling. I shouldn't spend all of my time with him. He'll just think he's extra special or something. He's not. He's just a guy. Just a fake summer fling.

"I need a new boyfriend," Kylie says as she drives around the mall parking lot, trying to find a closer spot to park. Kylie's hair and makeup are done up to perfection today and she doesn't want a long parking lot walk in the sun to melt her beauty.

"I'm glad you're officially over Trey, but do you want to dive back into a relationship again?" I say it because I need to. That's the type of thing I always say. If I'm being honest though, I'd tell her yes! That boyfriends are great and being all stupidly mushy gushy around a guy who likes you back is the greatest feeling ever. But I can't say any of that because she doesn't know about Liam. Therefore I have to keep acting like my normal self and my normal self would warn her to take a breather from guys.

If she saw that photo on social media that angered my brother, she didn't say anything. The good news is that Kylie doesn't follow much motocross stuff online, so she probably didn't see it.

I did, however, get several texts from Rachael and Jodi, inquiring about the photo. They believed me when I said it was just an "inside joke" that someone photographed at the wrong moment.

My brother Brent, however, did not believe the same lie. He yelled at me for ten minutes over the phone and then lectured me for half an hour when I got back home. He tried to package his anger as just "looking out for me" but I know that deep down he just hates Liam. He doesn't really care about me, or about not wanting me to get hurt. My brother's reaction to this whole thing has been the one huge bummer to my otherwise amazing summer.

Kylie finally finds a spot to park and we make our way to the mall. "I just hate being single," she says. "I don't need a *relationship*, relationship. I just need something fun. Something that makes me feel confident again."

I take in the sight of her, in beautiful makeup and a gray sundress that hugs her curves and is accented with some black strappy sandals.

"You could have told me we were dressing to pick up guys," I say, looking down at my pathetic outfit of jean shorts and a t-shirt.

"You should *always* act like you're dressing to pick up guys," Kylie says.

I roll my eyes. "You are pathetic. And boy crazy"

She scoffs playfully, then turns her eyes on me and

wiggles her eyebrows. "Guess it's easy to stop caring about finding a boyfriend when you have Liam at your disposal."

"Huh?" I say, my heart pounding. "What do you mean?"

She shrugs. "You hang out with that boy at the track every day and he's the hottest thing ever. You really need to hook up with him."

I let out an internal sigh of relief. She doesn't know about us. Good.

And then I'm a little offended. "Since when am I a girl who just hooks up with guys?"

She snorts out a laugh. "You know what I mean… I'm not calling you easy or anything. But he's so cute and you're always hanging out."

We walk into the Starbucks inside the mall because Kylie always wants her caffeine fix before a shopping trip.

"We're just friends," I say. I hate how many times I've said that sentence. "We don't hang out… we ride at the same track. Like friends."

"Oh yeah?" Kylie says. She gives me a flirty look. "Prove it."

"How am I supposed to prove that we're just friends?" But before I've even finished my sentence, Kylie is turning her head toward the left side of the room and giving me eyes that says I should follow her gaze. There are two guys sitting next to each other, staring at the same laptop screen. Looks like they're studying for school or something.

I look back at Kylie. "You already found a guy you like?"

"No," she says softly as she grabs my arm. "I found *two* guys I like. One for me and one for you." She wiggles her eyebrows. "Which one do you want? They're both gorgeous, but I have a feeling about the one in the red shirt."

"Red Shirt is all yours," I say as we move forward in the coffee line. I glance over at them, not that I'm actually going to choose one to flirt with or anything—I just want to humor my best friend. "They're both pretty cute," I say. And they are, but they've got nothing on Liam.

The guy in the red shirt has dark skin and short hair, and he looks like he works out. The other guy next to him has light brown hair that's a little scruffy, and he's fit but in an athlete way, not like someone who frequently hits the gym to bulk up. They've both chosen iced tea as their drink of choice and they're talking softly to each other while they look at the computer.

"They look busy," I say. "They probably don't want anyone bothering them."

"Guys always want to be bothered," Kylie says. She orders our drinks, choosing the java chip frappuccino for both of us and then she insists on paying for mine since she has a gift card. Both of Kylie's parents are teachers, and their house is filled with Starbucks gift cards since that's what parents and students always give them for the holidays.

"Let's get our flirt on," she says, winking at me as we take our drinks a few minutes later.

I feel dumb, but I follow my best friend as she weaves through the other patrons and walks right up to the guys. "Mind if we join you?" she says. I admire her cool, confident demeanor. Of course, if I looked that awesome in her dress, I'd probably feel more confident, too.

The guys look up, and the red shirt one smiles. "Of course."

We sit down and Kylie flashes me this "told you so" look while she sucks on her straw. "I'm Kylie," she says, sliding her chair closer to Red Shirt. She's staked her claim on him, and he doesn't seem upset about it at all. "And this is my best friend, Bella."

"Hi there, Isabella," the other guy—the one with a black shirt—says. "It's nice to meet you. I'm Anthony."

"Bella," I say. "It's just Bella."

He smiles, revealing slightly crooked bottom teeth and he leans back in his chair. "Cool. You can call me Tony."

"Her name is actually Bella," Kylie says, not taking her flirty eyes off Red Shirt. I think he introduced himself but I wasn't paying attention. "Her parents put Bella on her birth certificate."

"No way? That's cool," Tony says. He gives me a bashful grin, but I can tell he's just doing it to be funny. "Sorry I called you the wrong name."

I smile. "It's fine."

"So what are you boys working on?" Kylie says. She is definitely sucking on her straw in a way that's supposed to catch a guy's attention. I want to tell her we get it. She's flirting. It's obvious. The entire coffee shop is aware of it by now.

"We're working on an app," Red Shirt says. "It's almost ready, just getting a few bugs out."

"We're gonna get rich off it," Tony says.

"What's the app about?" I ask.

Tony slides his chair a little closer. "I don't want to bore you," he says. His eyes drop down, giving me a once over before they meet my gaze again. "Tell me about yourself."

Before long, Tony and I have talked about every possible topic under the sun, while my best friend flirts her butt off with Ray, which I finally figure out is Red Shirt's real name.

I'm not having fun at first, but then the attention is actually kind of cool. Guys never really paid attention to me in high school, and it's just harmless flirting, so who cares?

Plus, I'm not laying it on thick. I'm just being myself. But beside me, Kylie has had her arm playfully resting on top of Ray's arm for a while now.

After our coffees are empty, Kylie suggests walking around the mall. She's practically glued to Ray's side and I'm surprised she hasn't found a flirty way to slide her hand into his by now. Kylie really has a way with guys, and every time she's set her sights on one, she ends up dating him. I wonder what she'd say if she knew that her best friend is currently in the middle of a fun fling with Liam Mosely. Too bad I'm not going to share that juicy secret.

"Your friend really digs Ray," Tony says while we walk a few feet behind them.

I snort. "She came here hoping to find someone."

"What about you?" he asks. "Did you want to find someone?"

I don't know how to answer. If I tell him I have no interest in finding a boyfriend because I already have a summer fling all lined up, who knows how he'd react. I don't want to lead him on, but I also just don't know what to say. Tony is nice. He's been a gentleman so far, which is more than I can say for a lot of guys who meet you and then try shoving their tongue down your throat thirty seconds later. But I don't feel any exhilarating rush of excitement when I talk to Tony. His eyes don't make my stomach hurt in a good way. Being near him doesn't make my heart pound. When I look at him, I just see a regular guy.

When I look at Liam—well, I see someone I want to be close to. I feel like I'm floating on air, and drowning in happiness. There's a magnetic connection there, something I can't hold back from, even though I know it doesn't matter because Liam can never officially be mine. Maybe Tony could be mine... if I flirted with him more or gave him an opportunity to make a move.

Would I want that if Liam wasn't here this summer? Would I be excited about the possibility of dating Tony?

"Oooh," Ray says, walking up to a shoe store. "They finally got my kicks in stock."

"Uh oh," Tony says, flashing me a smile. "He's going to be a while."

My phone rings just as everyone is walking into the store.

I check the screen and see Liam's number. "I'll be right in," I tell them as I walk over to a nearby bench and sit down.

"Hey," I say, answering the call. "Are you feeling okay?"

"I'm a little better," Liam says. "How's best friend day going?"

I sigh. "She found a guy after about three seconds. We've spent the entire time with them."

"Them?"

"Yeah, Kylie's new guy has his friend with him so we're all just hanging out. I think Kylie thinks she's doing me a favor by forcing me to hang out with some guy."

"Is it working?" he asks. And the weird thing is that I don't hear any hint of jealousy in his voice.

"I think he likes me," I admit. "But I don't care."

"Well if he's a good guy, you should go for it."

My heart skips a beat. "You want me to date someone else?"

"Eh," he says. "I don't get to stop you, Bella. I'm just the fling, remember?" He chuckles like it's no big deal. "If you wanna date the guy, go for it."

I swallow, and the world seems to fade away all around me. I can't believe what I'm hearing. Liam isn't jealous. He doesn't care that he's home sick and I'm spending time with a new guy. I really am just a fling to him.

I guess I knew it all along, but it hurts to find out for sure.

I take a deep breath. "I better get back to my friends."

8

LIAM

There's a light tap on my door and then a paper slides underneath the bottom crack. I get up and walk over to see the next installment of Liam's Motocross Adventures, a hand-drawn comic book authored by my little stepbrothers. Since my mom banned them from seeing me this week so they wouldn't get sick, they've taken it upon themselves to entertain me by making these comic books. They're each about six pages long, drawn on computer paper that's then been folded in half and stapled to look like a book. So far there's been five "issues" of these mini-comic books, and they all star me, a famous dirt bike racer who goes on adventures. My character has defeated dinosaurs, dragons, Fortnite, and our mom's broccoli soup that was struck by lightning and became sentient and tried to kill the whole family until I destroyed it by driving my dirt bike over the mutant broccoli.

I didn't realize little kids could be so creative. I'm going to keep these little handmade books forever.

"Thanks, guys," I call out through the closed door as I pick up issue number six. This one is called Liam Gets Sidekicks, and judging by the two kids drawn on the cover, they've inserted themselves into this story.

"This is our favorite one!" Dylan says through the door.

"Mom wants to know if you want some ice cream?" Matt says.

"Yes please," I call back through the door as I make my way back to my bed to read the new comic book.

It's Friday, and I feel better today than I have all week. My aches and pains are gone, and my fever has been gone for a full twenty-four hours. Now, the only thing that's truly bothering me are thoughts of Bella.

She went to the mall the other day and told me about this guy who was hitting on her. I knew this day would come, when some local guy would catch her eye and he could give her everything I can't. A real relationship. I had hoped the day would come after I'd left Roca Springs, that way it wouldn't hurt me too badly.

But I didn't get that lucky. I did what I had promised myself I would do – let her go without drama. I hate it. I hate every second of it, but what else am I supposed to do? This is a summer fling. I can't just beg her to stay with me knowing I'll be leaving after the summer. I can't ask her to put aside her own life just because I'm selfish and want her all to myself.

Maybe this dude at the mall is supposed to be her soul mate. I can't stand in the way of that.

She hasn't told me anything else about him over the last two days, but it's not like I asked. We've texted a little bit, but she hasn't been by with any more chicken and dumplings. Not that I can blame her. She met a new guy. Why would she keep bringing food to her old summer fling?

Jealousy rockets through me and I set the comic book down. I can't attempt to read it when I'm feeling this awful.

My mom walks in and brings me a bowl of ice cream.

"What's this?" she says, picking up the comic book.

"The boys have been making them for me all week," I say.

She flips through it, her curiosity turning into a grin. "Aren't they just the sweetest things?"

"Yeah," I say. "I'm really glad you found Phil."

Mom smiles one of her tight-lipped smiles. I think she tries really hard to make sure she doesn't insult my father, but it doesn't bother me. He wasn't the best husband to her and he's not the greatest dad, either. He thinks throwing money at stuff will make it perfect, but that doesn't always work.

"Dad sucks," I say. "He only cares about work. Not you, not me. He wouldn't have done anything while I was sick. He might have left me some money to order pizza or something, but that's it. You're a really great mom and I'm sorry I haven't been around much."

Her smile wavers and the corners of her eyes crinkle. "Well, you're here now," she says, pressing the back of her hand to my forehead. "Your fever has been gone for over a day now. That's great."

"Am I no longer a prisoner in my own room?" I ask with a grin.

She laughs. "I suppose not. Just don't breathe too close to the boys. You might still be contagious."

With my newfound freedom, I wander out to the garage and look at my bike. I haven't ridden since last weekend. The last time I went this long without being on my bike was when I broke my arm three years ago. I was so sick for a few days this week that it didn't bother me, but now that I'm feeling better, I'm dying to get back on my bike.

It's Friday, which means it's race day, but I know I'm not ready to race right now. I'm still weak and tired and I'm not about to risk getting second place, or worse. If I'm not going to win, I'm not going to race. I have a reputation to uphold.

The garage door bursts open and Matt says, "Your phone is ringing!"

I head back inside to where I left my phone on the charger and see a missed call from Bella. Finally. I've missed her so much. I call her back.

"How are you feeling?" she asks.

"Better. No more fever or anything."

"That's awesome," she says. "Are you racing tonight?"

"Nah, I don't think I'm up to it. But if you're racing, I'll come cheer you on."

"I don't feel like racing tonight," she says. "I wanted to do something fun instead. Not that racing isn't fun but... you know what I mean. Something a different kind of fun."

"Oh, okay." My happiness wanes. I remember why we haven't talked much in the last few days. "You must have a hot date tonight."

She's silent for a beat. I guess I'm right. She's calling to tell me about the new guy she's dating.

"Well, I'm *trying* to get a hot date," she says. "But he hasn't asked me yet."

"Maybe you should ask him." I absolutely hate giving her dating advice. If I had it my way, she wouldn't see anyone else but me.

"I was hoping I could just hint about wanting to do something fun and maybe he'd ask me first," she says. There's a subtle playfulness in her voice.

"Wait..." I say. "Who are we talking about here?"

She laughs. The sound of her laughter brings me back to all the amazing days we've had together this summer. I can picture her, head thrown back, laughing up at the sky at something stupid I said. My heart aches for this girl. More than she'll ever know.

"I'm talking about you, dummy."

I swallow. "You want me to ask you out?"

"Duh."

"What about that guy from the mall?"

"He's not you," she says, and my heart instantly warms up. "So, Liam? You going to ask me out or what?"

I grin. "Would you like to go out and do something fun with me tonight?"

"Yes," she says. "I thought you'd never ask."

I PICK HER UP AN HOUR LATER AFTER I'VE SHOWERED AND FIXED my hair and assured myself that I look good, and not like someone who was sick all week. I feel good, so that makes me halfway there. The anticipation of seeing Bella again has the power to eradicate any sickness that's still lingering in my body. She's the bright spot on any gloomy day.

There are only a few fun things to do in Roca Springs, and I've decided on an outdoorsy activity for our date today. This thing with Bella feels more important than some lame date to the movies. I want to do something gutsy and extreme with her. Like the sport of motocross, only different.

"Are we going to the rock?" Bella says when I turn down the little road that leads to the state park on the outskirts of town.

"Yep," I say. "Is it that obvious?"

She grins. "I'm excited. I haven't been since I was thirteen and I was too chicken to walk to the top."

"Well, we're going," I say as I pull into a spot to park. "All the way to the top."

She sucks in air through her cheeks and claps her hands. "I'm excited!"

The Rock was my mom's idea when I told her I needed a date idea that wasn't boring. It's a large, mountain of sorts that looks like a large concrete dome. It's round and smooth and not jagged like a real mountain. The attraction has been turned into a state park. Thousands of years of erosion has made the top surface smooth, and from a distance it looks like a big round rock. You can hike all the way up to the top and get a great view of the surrounding towns. I checked out the website for it, and once a month when it's a full moon, people like to camp out on top of the rock. Unfortunately for us, tonight is not a full moon. But I'm hoping it'll still be romantic. We still have a few hours of daylight left, which is good because I'm not sure I'd want to hike back down this huge rock with no light.

Bella watches me lean over the back of my truck. I take out my backpack and pull it on my shoulders.

"You came prepared," she says.

I grin. "Picnic dinner at the top of the rock. How's that for romance?"

She tucks her hair behind her ears. "I'm impressed."

There's a little gravel trail through the parking lot that leads to the base of the rock. We follow the wooden signs that lead us there. Bella walks up to me and loops her arm through mine. "I missed you this week. Don't ever get sick again."

"I will certainly try not to," I say with a laugh. "I can't remember the last time I've been that sick."

"Well, you're better now," Bella says, leaning her head against my arm while we walk. I breathe in the scent of her shampoo and I'm so glad to have her back with me. I can't stand the thought of her spending the day with some other guy at the mall. She should be with me, even if it isn't fair. Even if I'll be leaving and this is just a fling. She should be with me.

There's a half mile walk on flat ground before we get to the base of the Roca Springs Rock. Signs warn us to be careful along the way, but the walk up to the top is still considered a level three hike, and since the levels go up to seven, I'd say it should be easy.

"Are you scared?" Bella asks, giving me a flirty grin as she walks ahead of me on the trail. At the base of the rock is several smaller boulders that we have to step over as we make our way up the slow incline.

"Never," I say, flashing her a grin back.

I try not to stare at her backside like some caveman, but it's hard. She is rocking those spandex workout pants. I had warned her before we left today that she should wear good shoes and dress for a day outside. Now, I get to reap the benefits of her clothing choices. This girl is hot in every possible way.

The trail narrows as we go through some trees and small, craggy surfaces, and then soon we are on the bottom of the large rock. It slopes gently upward, and it's so high you can't see the top from down here.

I walk next to Bella until the surface gets steep enough that it gets harder to walk.

"Why is this so hard?" Bella says, panting as she takes a long step upward.

"Turn sideways," I say, as I start walking diagonally up the surface instead of straight up.

"This is about where I chickened out last time," Bella says. She pauses and puts her hands on her hips and looks out at the view. It's beautiful up here, but there's still half of the rock to go. I want to see the top.

"Do you want to stop now?" I ask.

"Kind of…" she admits. Then she starts walking again. "But no."

"It plays tricks on you," I say as we keep scaling the large, impossibly huge rock. It's almost like we're on another planet that's crashed into earth and left a huge dome on the surface.

"It's such a gradual slope that if you fall you probably

won't even roll very far," I say, continuing to walk at an angle. "But it looks scary."

"Very scary," Bella says.

I reach behind me and hold out my hand. She takes it. We walk like this, hand in hand, slightly sideways as we wind our way up the sloping surface of the rock. I can see the crest at the top, where it levels out, next to a sign that's been driven into the rock.

A few minutes later, we're close enough to read what the sign says.

You've reached the summit of Roca Springs Rock. Elevation: 1,825 feet

I look back at Bella and squeeze her hand. "We did it."

She grins. "We made it to the top," she says, biting on her lip. "We still have to walk back down."

"That might be scarier," I agree. I turn to her and take out my phone. "Want to get a picture with the sign?"

"Totally," she says, grinning ear to ear.

We pose in front of it and I snap a selfie of us. I look like a huge dork in the photo because I'm accidentally staring at her. As soon as I put my phone back in my pocket, Bella reaches for my hand again.

"Don't let go. This is scary."

A gentle warm breeze floats across the rock as we turn and look out at the world below us. It's absolutely beautiful. Sloping land and towns as far as twenty miles away can be seen on the horizon. We've seen a few people walking on other parts of the rock, but right now we are the only people here. I hope it stays this way.

I turn toward her and circle my hands around her waist. She presses her head to my chest and closes her eyes.

"I wish summer flings lasted longer than the summer," she says.

"Me too," I say, kissing the top of her head.

BELLA

It's only when I close my eyes and hold onto Liam that I'm not scared. I can forget about the world around me, the terrifyingly long trip back down to solid ground, if I just breathe slowly and listen to the *thump, thump, thump* of Liam's heartbeat underneath his T-shirt. It's a soft cotton shirt, gray with a Fox head logo on the upper corner. And it smells like him. Or maybe that's just *him* that I smell. All woodsy and clean, even though it's hot outside and my forehead is beginning to sweat. He still smells amazing.

He lets me hold onto him for a long time, but eventually I need to pull away. There's only so long you can hug someone who isn't your official boyfriend while you're standing at the top of a huge rock.

I didn't tell him the whole truth about this stupid rock. He knows I'm a little scared of it, but the truth is - I am *terrified* of it.

I'm not a fan of heights, and I'm not a fan of trusting my own feet. Every step I took on the journey up here felt like a monumental task to force my body to keep its balance. I was so scared that I'd slip and fall and go tumbling down the rock, breaking every bone in my body along the way.

Riding dirt bikes and soaring ninety feet through the air? No problem.

But this rock? It's terrifying. That's why I never made it up here in all the times I've been here on field trips and weekend lunches with my friends. But for Liam, I'm willing to step outside of fear. He planned this date for us and for a few minutes in his truck today, I was about to tell him I didn't want to do it.

I step back, but still hold onto him as I turn and look around at the world below us. It's absolutely beautiful. The sky is a crystal blue with only a few white, puffy clouds. I see my town, and the next town over. Behind us is mostly vast stretches of Texas hill country, with the occasional house or farm peppered throughout.

"I'm so glad I came up here," I say, as I stand in awe of the beauty around me.

"Ready for lunch?" Liam asks. He slides off his backpack and kneels down as he unzips it. I stand here and watch him unfold a navy blue blanket onto the rock. Then, very carefully, I kneel down too, and sit on the blanket. My fear of heights lessens after I sit down. I feel safer on my butt. Less likely to fall.

"Okay, don't laugh but I did the best I could," Liam says. He takes a lunch kit out of his backpack and lays out the lunch he made for us. There's sandwiches, chips, strawberries, and cupcakes from the best bakery in town.

"You made us lunch?" I say, giving him a coy smile. "That is really sweet."

"Sweet or lame?" he says, handing me a soda. "I mean, I guess I could have gotten takeout or something?"

I shake my head. "No I like this. It's better than takeout. You put effort into it."

"That's my style," he says, cracking a grin. "I'm full of effort."

I know he doesn't mean anything by it, but just mentioning the word effort make me wonder why we can't just put in the effort to make this thing work. We don't have to be a fling – we could be something more… right? I don't say anything though. I know it would be pointless to bring it up. At best, he'd just laugh me off, but at worst, he'd think I'm some stalker girl who can't just be cool like I agreed to at the start of summer. I am not one of his obsessed fangirls. I can be cool.

So instead of voicing my desires, I eat lunch next to Liam on the soft fleece blanket while we gaze out at scenery.

Liam tells me about his week of being sick, and how his little brothers kept him entertained even though they couldn't go in his room.

"I missed you these last two days," Liam says during a moment of silence.

"Sorry," I say, taking a bite of my sandwich. "My brother was here using my mom's printer for his project. He's been coming home a lot lately and I hate it."

"Well, that's better than what I thought," Liam says. "I thought you had grown tired of me…started dating that other guy."

"Never!" I say, putting a hand on my chest in a dramatic way. "You're my favorite summer fling!"

"Good," he says with a grin. "You're my favorite, too."

"How many summer flings do you currently have?" I ask playfully.

He leans over and kisses my cheek. "Just you."

"How many did you have last summer?"

He takes a bite of his sandwich and watches me. "None. You're my first summer fling."

I don't want to admit how happy that makes me. Relieved, even. I shrug one shoulder. "First time for everything."

"Oh yeah?" he says, nudging me with his elbow. "How many summer flings have you had?"

"Just you." I set my sandwich down in my lap on top of the plastic wrap it came in. "I haven't dated much."

Liam's eyes feel like they're searching deep into my soul as he watches me. "Have you been in love before?"

I shake my head. "You?"

"Nah," he says, looking at his food. "I've had a few girlfriends. Nothing serious. Motocross is my true love."

I know I should probably keep my distance, seal up my heart and not reveal any of my deepest thoughts. But Liam isn't just some guy. He's my best friend lately. We've shared a lot with each other, including our saliva. So I don't hold back. "None of my past relationships were serious either. I've just had a series of guys who are into me for a week or two and then it's over. You've actually stuck around longer than anyone else."

He smirks. "Guess I'm the smartest one."

I change the subject, because talking about boyfriends and dating just makes my heart hurt. I know Liam will never be what I want him to be, and I know I agreed to this summer fling. It was my idea after all. I can't go getting sad about something that I wanted in the first place.

After lunch is over, we pack up our trash back into Liam's backpack and we hang out on the rock some more. It's afternoon now, and the sun is behind us, lighting up Roca Springs in a beautiful summery glow. Liam lays down on the blanket and I follow his lead. I lay down next to him, then slide over and snuggle on his chest, while his arm wraps around my shoulders.

It's the most intimate we've ever been, lying here like this. If we were in a bed, I'd feel intimidated. Thrilled. Scared. But we're out here in the wide open, laying on a massive rock that's open to other tourists, even though we haven't seen any in a while.

It feels safe lying here with Liam. I don't feel pressured. That's why, after about half an hour of staring out at the town below, I lean up on my elbow and look at him.

"What?" he says.

I lean forward and kiss him. His lips are warm from the sun, and they send a jolt of heat straight through my body. I feel his hands in my hair, and then sliding down my back as I deepen the kiss, feeling like if I just kiss him a little bit longer I'll be able to memorize every inch of him. Like I could find a way to keep him in my heart, forever and ever and then I can pull him out and relive these moments after he's gone.

Before I know it, I'm pulled on top of him, our bodies pressed close, our lips pressed closer.

My whole body is heated, and desperate. I like him so much more than I can ever admit. And yet… he's not mine. Not fully.

He's just here for the summer.

I pull away and slide off him, giving us several inches of space on the blanket. Liam takes a quick breath and blinks. "Whoa," he says, leaning up on his elbow. "I liked that."

"Summer will be over soon," I say. "We have just a few weeks left. What will happen then?"

I can feel them, the hot stinging tears of betrayal threatening to roll from my eyes. I try to hold them back because I cannot cry. Not here, not in front of the guy I'm pretending that I'm not totally falling for. Liam watches me with concern. He looks pained, and it's probably a reflection of my own expression right now.

"What are we going to do when summer is over?" I say, my voice coming out just above a whisper.

He leans forward and cups my chin in his hand. "Sweetheart, don't think like that. Let's just stay in our bubble of happiness right now."

"But this bubble won't last much longer," I say.

He shakes his head. "So why make it pop quicker than it needs to? You're here. I'm here. Let's not think about the future. Worrying about the end of summer will just make us hurt twice as much."

I swallow my pain and brush off the two stray tears that managed to fall down my cheek. I nod quickly. "You're right. There's still time."

"Come here," he says, wrapping an arm around my shoulders as he pulls me to him. I feel his lips press to the top of my head. "Don't cry, Bella. I don't ever want you to cry over me."

Then don't leave, I think.

But of course, I'm smart enough to keep my thoughts to myself

LIAM

On Monday morning I find myself in the Houston Intercontinental Airport. Phil was nice enough to drop me off on his way to work, even though it's an hour out of the way for him. He's a great guy. Seems like the longer I live with my mom and her new family, the more I regret staying away from them all these years. I could have been getting to know Phil and Matt and Dylan but instead I kept to myself in Houston and only cared about dirt bikes.

Could I still have been a professional racer if I'd spent more time in Roca Springs? My life would have surely been different. I could have grown up here, gone to school here, raced at the local track every weekend.

Maybe I would have met Bella years ago and our relationship would have been solid enough by now to survive what's coming next: Team Loco.

I got the call on Sunday night. Marcus told me I'd be flown into Cali in the morning to sign my Team Loco contracts for the next season and to get fitted for my bike and gear. It's all happening so fast now and there's still three weeks left of summer.

At any other point in my life, I'd be ecstatic for the events of today, but right now I'm wishing it could all wait a bit longer. I'm not ready to leave Bella and this charming little Texas town behind. I still want Team Loco more than anything, because this is my career. I have the potential to make a ton of money in just a decade of racing and then I could always come back here and see if Bella is still around.

Who am I kidding? She won't be here in ten years. She'll have been swept off her feet by some other charming guy, some guy who can provide her everything she needs here at home. Some guy who won't leave her every week to go race in another state.

I feel sick about it as I board my plane. I'm sitting next to an older woman who looks to be in her sixties or so. She stares at me as I store my suitcase in the overhead bin.

"You're a handsome fellow," she says when I sit down next to her.

I chuckle awkwardly. "Um, thank you."

"You got a lady at home?"

I could tell her the truth, but it's not like I'll ever see her again after this. I smile. "Yes, ma'am."

She nods as if she knew it all along. "She's a lucky girl."

"Thanks, but I'm the lucky one."

She smiles as if that was the right thing for me to say. She falls asleep shortly after the plane takes off, but I would have been fine if we'd spent the entire trip talking about Bella. My heart longs for her even now, and I saw her just last night. I don't know what I'll do when I have to leave for good.

Team Loco's headquarters is located in a fancy office building. I meet Marcus, who is wearing jeans and a suit jacket, which I guess is the ultra-tacky business-casual style here in Los Angeles. He shakes my hand and offers me a variety of snacks from the food table in the conference room.

Then the lawyers come in, two women, one of which I recognize as Mrs. Baker. She's married to a professional racer. Everyone is friendly and cordial and not one person I met today looks at me like I don't belong here with Team Loco. My past indiscretions are either forgotten or forgiven, and that's a relief. I feel the tightly wound ball of nerves in my stomach start to loosen as the day goes on. I had been prepared for a full on lecture about my conduct and the expectations of being a racer for Team Loco, but that doesn't happen. They treat me with respect, and that makes me respect them a whole lot more, too. Maybe Marcus understands that while I got kicked off Team FRZ Frame for fighting, it was only because the people I were fighting were bad people – not me.

Regardless, now I'm more motivated than ever to make Team Loco my official home team. I'll surpass their expectations in the coming racing season and they'll eagerly sign me on for next season as well. I'll make my career, right here, with the fantastic people of Team Loco.

After a brief explanation of all the paperwork in front of me, I sign my contracts, making me an official rider for the fall racing season. Marcus claps me on the back. "We're happy to have you, son."

"Thank you, sir," I say, wondering if it would be silly to keep the pen I signed my contracts with as a souvenir. "I'm really happy to be here."

"Ready for the fun part?" he asks.

I lift an eyebrow. "This wasn't the fun part?"

Marcus stands and I stand too. "Not even close," he says as he leads me out of the conference room and down the hallway.

The next room looks completely out of place for an upscale office building, and I'm digging it. It's filled with racing gear. Jerseys, pants, boots, helmets—everything.

A guy with bright blue hair that's gelled into a mohawk stands and shakes my hand. "Hey there. You must be Liam?"

"That's me," I say.

"Cool, cool. Good to meet you. I'm Zo. Like Jo, but with a Z. Let's get you fitted."

He makes me stand on a small podium thing that's about six inches off the floor. Then he uses the tape measure that hangs around his neck and measures all over my body.

"I didn't realize the riding gear was customized," I say while he's measuring the length of my arm.

"Oh yes," Zo says. "We want our men looking good. And you, sir, look good." He winks at me.

I try on boots to find my size, and then do the same thing with the gloves and helmets. Zo marks it all down in my file and then I'm shuffled off to the next room, which looks even more out of place than the last one.

It's like an upscale mechanic shop in here. The floor is tiled with black and white tiles, and the walls are painted a deep Team Loco blue. There are several brand new Team Loco dirt bikes lined up in here.

"Hey, man, how's it going?" a guy says. He's probably in his thirties, and he's covered in tattoos. From a first glance, they all look dirt bike related, except for the tattoo of a beautiful woman on his bicep.

He shakes my hand. "I'm Trevor. Lead Mechanic. I'll be seeing a lot of you this season."

"Sounds good. I'm looking forward to being on the team."

Trevor points to a scale on the floor. "Hop on."

I stand on the scale and he marks my weight on a notebook. "How tall are you?"

"Six one."

He marks that, too. Then I sit on the display bikes and he measures my body on the bike. This kind of attention to detail is what makes an amateur rider turn into a pro.

My new Team Loco bike will be customized to fit me perfectly. The suspension will be matched to my weight and height, giving me the fastest bike possible. After chatting about bikes with Trevor for a bit, I'm told that the rest of Team Loco will be here soon and we'll go out to lunch.

I slip into the lobby and call Bella just because I'm missing her voice.

"Hey," she says, answering after several rings. "I'm with Kylie. We're headed to the movies."

"Does that mean you can't talk?" I ask.

"Sort of," she says. "What's up?"

I don't know why she hasn't trusted Kylie with our summer fling status, but I respect it. I tell her about my experience in LA so far and how great everything's been. She only answers in quick, one word replies that won't give away who she's talking to if Kylie is listening in. If we were actually dating, this wouldn't be a problem. There wouldn't be any lies or secrets. But I can't dwell on that now.

"I miss you," I say.

"Uh huh," she says brightly.

"I miss you a lot," I say, just to tease her.

"Same here," she says.

I laugh. "I'll pretend that you said you miss me too, even though you won't dare say it out loud in front of Kylie."

"Thanks," she says. "I'll call you after the movie?"

"Please do," I say. Then I lower my voice, even though the lobby is empty. "I wish you were in my arms."

"Me too," she says, sounding flustered. Good. I like her flustered. "Talk to you later."

Shortly after my phone call, the elevator at the end of the hall opens and the famous Team Loco guys themselves walk out. Clay recognizes me first since we've already met at the track back in Roca. He's tall and tattooed, with short dark hair. "Hey, man," Clay says, walking up and fist-bumping me a hello. "Good to see you."

I meet Jett Adams next, who was the youngest Team Loco racer until they hired me. He comes from a motocross family. His dad raced professionally when he was younger and now they own a dirt bike track a few hours away from Roca Springs in Texas.

Jett shakes my hand. "I'm glad to pass on my rookie hat to you," he says with a laugh. "Prepare for a crap ton of press and interviews asking if you feel intimidated about being so young."

"Good to know," I say.

"The PR can be a nightmare for all of us," Aiden Strauss says. He's slightly shorter and stockier than the other guys, with dark tan skin and dark hair. "Glad to have you on the team," he says. "I've seen you ride and you're lightning fast."

"I appreciate that," I say.

The last member of Team Loco is Zach Pena. He was the team's so-called bad boy a few years ago. Now he's straightened up and he's a solid role model for kids. From what I remember of my internet research on the team, Zach is the oldest member, at twenty-three.

"How's my team doing?" Marcus calls out as he leaves his office. "Ready for dinner?"

"Avery got us reservations at your favorite place," Clay says.

Marcus puts a hand to his chest. "Bless that girl. She's my favorite employee, you know."

I'm not sure what all they're talking about, or what this favorite restaurant is, but I'm happy to be included. We head downstairs where a limo is waiting for us.

"We don't always ride in limos," Jett tells me as we pile into the car. "Just occasionally when we're celebrating something."

"What are we celebrating?" I ask.

He laughs. "You."

The rest of the day is straight up amazing. I'm hanging out with four professional motocross racers, my new boss, and I'm in the beautiful city of Los Angeles. It's easy to get caught up in our fame after a few people recognize us and ask for photos.

But after a few hours, I find myself longing for Bella. Wishing I could call her. Wishing I could go home to be with her.

And then I have to stop myself. I keep thinking about how badly I want to go home. But home isn't Roca Springs. It's Houston.

I'm not sure when it happened, but at some point, my own home in Houston doesn't feel like it's actually my home anymore.

When I think of home, I think of that spare room filled with Mom and Phil's junk and the twin bed that I sleep on next to a suitcase of my clothes.

When I think of home, I think of Bella.

BELLA

$\mathcal{I}$ think I understand my best friend better now that I have this thing with Liam. Before, when I was single and alone, I hated when she would date someone and run off and spend all her free time with him. Now, I get it. When you like someone, you just want to be around them. I'm having the hardest time being away from Liam while he's in California, and while I like hanging out with my best friend, it's also boring. Everything we do feels less exciting when my heart is too busy longing after a guy.

I keep wanting to be with him, not seeing movies with Kylie. I want to snuggle against his chest and immerse myself in his scent instead of painting my nails with Kylie. I think this makes me a bad friend. Or maybe boy crazy. But I'm not doing much to stop it. I think about Liam all day, every day, even though I'm making sure to spend time with Kylie in these few days that he's gone. I haven't seen her much lately and I need to make up for being an absent friend, especially since she has no idea that I'm secretly seeing someone. At least when Kylie ditches me, I know it's because of a guy.

Right now, she must think I've been a flaky friend all summer.

This whole summer fling thing is not the laid back fun thrill I thought it would be. After Kylie and I have spent the day together, we go our separate ways. Kylie has to babysit her brothers tonight, and normally I'd offer to hang out with her. Instead, I'm eager to get back home so I can talk to Liam once he's back to his hotel today. I've only heard snippets of his day through texts, and it sounds exciting.

He texts me around dinner time and tells me to watch a famous motocross YouTube channel because they're about to broadcast live.

Me: You're going to be on TV?

Liam: yes ma'am :)

I pull up the YouTube channel and watch their live feed. They're in LA, at some local motocross track, talking about the upcoming fall racing season. A woman named Krystal Jade is the host of the show, and she's dressed in a bikini top and cut off jean shorts that are so short they might as well be underwear. I roll my eyes. I'm not sure what a bikini has to do with motocross. Maybe that's how everyone in LA dresses all the time. It's definitely different than how we dress here in Texas.

"Now we're excited to chat with Team Loco and its newest member, Liam Mosely," she says as the camera pans over Liam and four other equally handsome guys. I can tell most of them apart now because after Liam told me about his Team Loco news, I looked up their website and social media pages. All four of the other guys are all in committed relationships. I wonder how they pull that off, especially since Liam doesn't even want to pretend to date me. We are solidly fling status and he doesn't want anything else out of me.

Krystal Jade introduces Liam, who smiles into the camera in a way that makes my knees weak. I wonder if the four hundred and twelve people who are also watching this live video are thinking the same thing? He answers some questions about motocross, and then the other guys talk as well. I don't pay much attention to what everyone else says, because my eyes never leave Liam. He looks so cool and collected while on camera. He doesn't seem nervous at all, and even though he's only just met the team today, he's already in sync with them. They stand around on the sidelines of this sunny motocross track and act like old friends. In the distance, eager fans mull around waiting for their chance to meet them.

It's a lot like when Liam is surrounded by fans here in town, but it's different. It's bigger. More important.

I knew it was a big deal that he got signed onto Team Loco. I knew his life would change and he'd start traveling and become a big shot celebrity. But it isn't until right now, as I watch him looking absolutely perfect on camera, that I realize exactly how much he will change. That's why he didn't want to date me in any serious capacity. This is why we've never talked about the idea of dating after summer is over. Liam's old small-town life with me is almost at an end.

In three weeks, the summer will be over and he'll be jet-setting around the country. This was never meant to last. Why did I ever allow my heart to think it would?

With a heavy sadness in my heart, I close off the web browser. I can't bear to watch him anymore. He's moving on. He's doing amazing things with his life. He's famous now. His future is destined to be great—so much better than anything I'll ever do.

I should stop spending my days daydreaming about a stupid boy who isn't even my boyfriend. Anger and shame roll over me. How could I have been so stupid? Why did I eagerly give up my entire summer just to swoon over Liam Mosely? It's been a total waste.

I should have been figuring out my own life so that I can do something fun, *be* something fun. I don't want to be stuck in this small town forever, and yet for the last two months, I've been living my life as if that's exactly what I planned to do.

I open another web browser and start searching for Texas colleges. I've been down this road a hundred times, but it's never made any sense to me. I don't know what I want to do for a career. I don't know what I should go to college for, or if I should even *go* to college. So many of the people I went to school with had already figured everything out long before graduation. They were applying for colleges in their junior year, securing scholarships before Christmas break. They acted like college was the most important thing on earth, and I just rolled my eyes and figured it didn't matter that much. I've never had a plan. Never known what my future holds.

Maybe it's time I figure that out. I will go to school and make something of myself. While Liam is traveling and becoming a celebrity, I'll be moving on, too. He'll be just a blip in my past, nothing special. Just like how I'll soon be just a blip in his past. I bet he won't even remember me after a few weeks of his new life.

These realizations hurt me, and I tell myself to toughen up. I knew this was in the cards. I'm the one who even suggested the stupid summer fling in the first place. I'm not allowed to be heartbroken now. I signed up for it, after all.

That's why I won't be heartbroken. I refuse. I'm going to move on now instead of dragging it out into a painful end. Starting with college.

"Knock, knock," my mom says as she taps lightly on my open bedroom door.

"Come in," I say.

"Just wanted to see if you want pizza for dinner."

"Always," I say with a laugh.

"*Ooh*, colleges," Mom says when she sees my laptop screen. "Are you figuring out what you want to do?"

I shrug. "I don't know. Maybe. I'm trying."

Mom chuckles. "Anything I can help with?"

I shrug again. "I don't know. I have no idea what I want to do."

"I'm no stranger to that," she says, brushing my hair back behind my ears. My mom was a stay at home mom when she was married to my dad. After they divorced, she got a quick job at a restaurant, just until she found something else to do. She ended up working there for a few years and moving up to manager. Now she works in the restaurant chain's corporate office downtown. She never even got a college degree, but she does take night classes now that her work pays for.

"There's no rush to figure out what you want to do," Mom says. "Brent says he wants to work in finance, but I'll believe it when I see it. I think he just wanted a cool sounding major so he could impress girls." She winks at me. I hate to say it, but I think she's right. I can't picture my athletic brother wearing a suit and tie to go work in some stuffy office.

"I have no idea what I want to do. Not even the slightest inkling. All career paths sound boring to me."

"Eh, you'll figure it out," Mom says. "Maybe get your first two years done at the community college, and then you might have a better idea of career options after that."

I nod. "That's a good idea."

It's a safe idea. The cheaper idea. It would be boring, but it would be something. Of course that's the problem… I don't want to be boring. Liam is going to be living this amazing life filled with motocross and fame and money. I'll be back here in Roca Springs, being a pathetic loser. I want to be passionate about something in the way he is about professional motocross. Sure, I love my bike and I love riding, but I'm no pro. I wouldn't know the first thing about going professional, and I'm probably too old to start out anyway. That's not the life I want. I don't want fame and fans. I just want something that will feel like I'm not some small-town loser.

"I'll go order the pizza," Mom says before leaving my room. I look back at my computer and go to the local community college website. I remember hearing my mom and my brother argue about community college. She wanted him to attend because it was right down the road and it's way cheaper than university. But Brent wanted the university experience. He wanted dorm rooms and student loans. I think I'll be fine with community college, so long as I can do something fun with my life.

After dinner, I'm still trying to figure it out. There's only so many ways you can Google the phrase "what should I do with my life" before you realize that the internet might not have all the answers.

Liam calls me around ten o'clock at night, which is only eight in California time. I want to hear his voice and fall asleep to him telling me all about his day. But that's something would make it harder to say goodbye at the end of summer. He's a fling, after all. I don't need to talk to him every day.

I let the phone call go to voicemail even though it hurts to miss out on an opportunity to talk to him. I need to stop relying on Liam to bring me happiness.

I need to start finding it for myself.

LIAM

Team Loco puts me up in a five-star hotel which is so nice I feel like I shouldn't be in here. Like maybe my mere presence will mess up the high-class luxury in this place. It has a hot tub and a shower and a balcony that overlooks Beverly Hills. The room always smells luxurious, if that's even a thing. Like lavender and money. I take pictures of the room and I wish I could tell Bella but she didn't answer my call last night. Or the night before. I worried that maybe my phone somehow didn't work this far from Houston, but I can call my mom just fine. It's Bella who isn't picking up.

In the morning, I gather my stuff and get some cinnamon flavored coffee from the hotel's lobby before I check out. Marcus calls me and wishes me a safe flight, and tells me they've arranged for a driver to take me to the airport. I'm really going to like being a part of Team Loco. They treat their people like royalty. Team FRZ Frame never did anything like this for me. They emailed my contracts and I had to sign them and email them back. With Team Loco, I got an all expenses paid trip to LA. Pretty awesome.

Now I'm even more determined to prove that I'm the racer they know I can be. I will stay on my best behavior and I will race with everything I've got. Just like Jett Adams, I'll bring them the podium wins this season. My flight back to Texas goes quickly, and soon we're landing and I'm eagerly taking my phone off airplane mode.

I wait a few minutes, watching my notifications pop up, hoping in vain that one of them will be from Bella. But there's nothing from her. It's been two days. This has officially moved past the territory of me just being paranoid. She's avoiding me.

I grab my suitcase and haul it off the airplane. I text Phil that my plane arrived on time and I walk out to find him waiting in the pickup line.

Before I get to the doors, I see two poster board signs that are wiggling excitedly from the two boys holding them. My mom, Phil, and the boys are all here, waiting for me.

The two poster board signs have been decorated in Matt and Dylan's signature comic book style. They've drawn me on a dirt bike, soaring over a jump, with my hands in the air in celebration. Off to the side, there's a stick figure holding a checkered flag.

Along the top of the sign are the words:

Welcome home Liam Mosely, bigshot professional racer

I can't help but laugh.

Mom hugs me. "How was your trip? Tell us all about it."

"Do you like our signs?" Matt says.

"I love them," I say, ruffling his hair.

"We're going to hang them on your bedroom wall," Dylan says.

"Cool." I don't bother telling him that the room I'm staying in isn't exactly my bedroom so I don't get to decorate it as if it were. It's the office with a bed in it. My mom might toss the poster boards long after I'm gone, but the boys don't need to know that.

We go out to eat and I tell them everything about my trip. It's hard to focus about all the exciting Team Loco things because I can't stop checking my phone, hoping for a text from Bella. My mind runs through all the situations that might have caused this lack of communication.

Maybe her phone broke?

But it's been two days. She would have gotten a new one or texted me from a friend's phone, or something. She could have emailed me to tell me her phone broke.

Maybe she's sick.

Maybe she got the flu from me and she's been in bed sick… but that wouldn't have stopped her from sending a text.

Maybe it's that guy she met at the mall. Maybe he took her on a date and she's in love with him now.

My stomach twists into knots. I don't want Bella to move on, not yet. I know she'll find a better guy after I'm gone and that's good—I want her to be happy. But I don't want to lose her yet. I still have three weeks.

Dinner is good, and my family is great, but it's a struggle to get through the meal without letting them know I'm freaking out on the inside. I put on a smile and answer my brother's questions and try to act normal.

They're all fascinated by the custom riding gear and custom bike I'll get now that I'm a member of Team Loco. Phil and the boys don't know much about motocross at all. My mom knows just enough because I grew up in this world, but she's always distanced herself from the sport. Now, they all look on eagerly while I explain how professional motocross works.

"Do you get paid too?" Dylan asks.

I grin. "Yep. It's a job. But I only get paid for each season and they only hired me on for one season so far."

"How much do you get paid?" Matt asks.

"It's rude to ask about money, son," Phil says.

I shrug. "It's a pretty standard contract. All rookies make the same amount."

My mom looks up, curiosity painted on her features. "A hundred grand," I say, answering her unasked question.

Her eyes widen. "Liam Mosely," she says, putting a hand to her chest. "Are you seriously getting paid that much?"

I can't tell if she's mad or happy, or just too surprised to smile. "Yes," I say. "I have the check in my backpack."

"Holy sh—" she breathes, stopping herself before cursing in front of the children. She grabs my hand. "No way."

I laugh. "Yes, Mom. That's why I've worked so hard to go pro. The money is worth it. And that's just rookie salary. If I stay on, I'll be making way more than that."

"Good job, Liam," Phil says. "I'm proud of you."

Mom's eyes tear up. "Oh honey," she says, pulling me into a side hug while we sit at this restaurant table. "I'm so, so proud of you."

She doesn't elaborate but I can see it in her eyes. She's thinking that she finally gets it now. The reason I dedicated so much of my life to the sport. The reason I let it take over my world. The money will be worth it. All of this hard work will result in being financially set for life, should I manage to stay on the team and not get hurt.

This is what I've worked so hard for, and now I've got it. The check is in my backpack. I've signed on the dotted line. I start racing for Team Loco in two weeks.

All of my wildest dreams have come true and yet I'm not as happy as I should be because I'm missing the girl who hasn't been answering my calls.

After dinner, there's still some time left before the motocross track closes for the day. If she's anywhere, she's there. I load up my bike and head out to Roca Sprigs Motocross Park, eager to see her. Maybe it'll all be a misunderstanding and maybe she's still mine, if only for a couple of weeks. I long for it to be true. I *need* it to be true. I'm not ready to say goodbye to her just yet.

I drive down the track, carefully looking at each truck in the parking lot. She's not by our tree, which is the only place she ever parks. Still, I refuse to give up hope until I've searched the entire facility. But her old black Chevy truck isn't here. I don't have the heart to ride my bike tonight, so I turn around and drive back home, defeated. Hurt. Heartbroken.

I can try to make excuses all I want. I can imagine scenarios where her phone broke and she's been trying to contact me but can't.

But deep down I know that's not true. Something happened between the time I got on the plane and when I got home.

Bella Castro doesn't care about me anymore.

13

BELLA

I can't take it anymore. I thought I could cut him off cold turkey, but I can't. Liam is my drug. He's also my friend. We've spent all of summer hanging out nearly every day at the track. I can't just drop it all because my feelings are hurt.

I text him on Saturday morning. I know he's back home because he tried calling me and left me a voicemail after he arrived back in town. I'm afraid he might be mad at me for ignoring him, but he answers on the first ring.

"Hey, stranger."

I swallow. *Busted.* "Hi."

"What's been going on?"

I can feel the tension in the air, the awkwardness between us that I personally put there by ghosting him for three days. I sigh. "I'm sorry, Liam. I was ignoring you."

"Yeah… I figured that much," he says. "Any reason why?"

"I'm just not ready for the fake breakup. I know it's coming after summer and when I saw you on YouTube it hit me that you're famous and I'm not. You've got a future and I don't."

"That's not true," he says. "You have whatever future you want."

"Not whatever future," I mumble. The future where Liam and I are together and happy doesn't exist in this world, only in my dreams.

"Look," he says softly. "We still have time. Let's not throw away our fling just yet. How about we go on a date today?"

I should say no. I shouldn't have called him. I should just stay away.

But my voice betrays my heart. "What did you have in mind?"

"Houston Comicpalooza."

"Houston what?" I say.

He laughs. "It's like the Comic Con of Texas. A huge superhero, super nerd convention. It's fun."

"It's two hours away." I say.

"Then we better get going."

I tell my mom I'm going to the Comicpalooza event with "some friends" and she just tells me to have fun. I don't get the third degree of questioning now that I'm eighteen. Since Brent isn't home, I let Liam come pick me up at my house, but I wait for him at the end of my driveway. No need for my mom to accidentally meet him. It's not like he's a real boyfriend after all.

Liam is wearing jeans and a Captain America T-shirt that hugs his muscles as if he were Chris Evans himself.

"Look at you, all nerded out," I tease as I climb into the passenger seat.

"No worries, I got one for you." He tosses a black shirt at me. I hold it up and see the same Captain America shield emblazoned on the front. I grin.

"Don't look," I say. Liam holds up one hand to block me from his view while he drives and I quickly slip out of my shirt and into this new one from Liam. It's brand new but has a hint of Liam's intoxicating scent on it.

When I'm done I turn toward him. "How do I look?"

"Like a very beautiful avenger," he says with a grin that makes my toes tingle.

The two-hour drive to Houston seems to take no time at all. I'd been a little worried that we wouldn't know what to talk about, but I was wrong. Liam and I fit together perfectly. Either as friends, or lovers. Doesn't matter. There are never awkward silences with us.

He tells me about Team Loco, but he keeps it brief and I'm grateful for that. I think it's extremely cool that he's an official pro racer again but I don't want details about the life he's going to have once he leaves me this summer.

I tell him about my friend Rachael who also rides dirt bikes but has been out of town at her dad's house this summer and how she really wants to meet him.

"Maybe we can all go out to dinner or something," Liam suggests.

I look down at our hands, which have been clasped together since we left Roca Springs. I don't even remember doing it—who reached over and grabbed the other's hand. It just comes naturally when we're alone.

I bite my lip. "We can totally hang out with my friends but just *as friends*," I warn. "No one knows that we're doing this… this fling thing."

"Got it," he says. "No flirting with you. Maybe I should flirt with your friends to throw him off the scent of us?"

I give him a look and he laughs. "I'm just playing."

Houston is a massive city that I haven't been to in a long time. We have to park several blocks away for the convention because it's so jam-packed with comic book fans. Liam and I walk hand in hand toward the convention center, passing hundreds of people in full on Cosplay outfits. Some of the costumes look amazing, and some are silly. Some people dress up as superheroes and others dress as obscure characters from lesser known TV shows. It all looks like fun, though.

The convention center has three floors of activities. The bottom floor is full of vendors selling every comic type thing you can think of, and Liam and I spend an hour wandering through them, but we haven't seen even half of what they have to offer yet. There are celebrities in attendance too, from movie stars to TV stars to the people who do the voices on cartoons and anime. You can get their autographs, take pictures with them, or watch them talk on panels.

Liam and I are totally out of our element here, but we're having a blast just looking at everything.

I get to sit in an actual helicopter, and he makes me take a photo of him in front of the car from the show Supernatural.

We eat nachos and get slushies and sit in the audience of panels that feature some extremely famous movie stars. Maybe it's because we're surrounded by all this other fame, but no one recognizes Liam. We are just two regular people here, holding hands and enjoying the show. It's like motocross and my hometown and my brother no longer exist while we're here. We get to be ourselves.

From an outsider I bet we look like a happy couple. Not a fake summer fling that is about to be over for good. From an outsider's perspective, I bet our lives look ideal.

We spend all day walking around, taking pictures, meeting people, and seeing cosplay contests. Soon my feet are aching from all the walking, and I'm hungry again.

"I have an idea," Liam says. "There's a pizza place right next to my house. Let's go get a slice."

"You live around here?" I ask.

He nods, his eyes brightening. "Yes, ma'am. Like four blocks down."

"But we're in the middle of the city," I say, gazing up at the skyscrapers as we step outside. "Does anyone actually *live* here?"

He chuckles. "My dad and I live in one of these high-rises." He points to the left to a white building that stands tall against the Houston skyline. "My dad designed it. It's all luxury condos."

'Wow," I say. "That's about as opposite as you can get from a life in Roca Springs."

"Tell me about it." He squeezes my hand. "Let's go."

Liam's building has its own parking garage in the lower levels, and he gets in with an access card on his dash. Even the parking garage is fancy looking. We park in his designated spot and he looks over and grins at me, pointing to the empty parking spot next to him. "My prayers have been answered. My dad isn't home. He's never home."

"I guess you don't want me to meet your dad the same way I don't want you to meet my mom."

"It's not the same," he says as we get out of the car and he reaches for my hand. "My dad is a prick. I'm not ashamed of you or anything, but I don't want to do that to you. He's not exactly friendly. I don't want you to meet him and think poorly of me."

"I know you, Liam. Your dad isn't going to change my opinion of you."

We step into an elevator and Liam presses the button for the fifteenth floor. Then he turns to me, placing his hands lightly on my hips.

"I missed you so much," he says softly, right before he kisses me.

The elevator takes off, making me lightheaded. Or maybe that's the power of Liam's kiss. Whatever it is, I wrap my arms around him and hold on tightly while we ascend to the fifteenth floor. My lips brush against his in a soft but passionate kiss. We've done this enough times that we're pros at it now, but then his tongue flicks across my bottom lip and it sends a shiver running straight down my body. I never get tired of kissing him.

The elevator slows to a stop and the doors click open, and we're forced to pull away. Liam gives me a sultry grin as he steps out of the elevator first.

I blink, my mind taking a second to adjust to the sight around me. I expected a hallway. But I'm standing in Liam's living room.

"You live on the whole floor?" I say, my jaw practically hitting the marble flooring.

"Yep," he says, tossing his keys into a glass bowl by the elevator. "This is my dad's domain. I just live in that room over there."

The elevator closes behind us and I whirl around to look at it. "But what if someone just walks into your house?"

He laughs. "You have to have a keycard to gain access to this floor. You must not have been paying attention when I used my card."

I blush from head to toe. "Well… no… I was preoccupied with you."

He touches my cheek and then plants a quick kiss on my forehead. "You're so cute when you're flustered. Come on, I'll give you the tour."

Liam's home has obviously been decorated by a professional. The place is luxury at its finest, and I feel a little silly for not realizing that he came from so much money. He doesn't talk about his dad much, besides telling me that he let him ride dirt bikes and that's why he lived with him after his parents' divorce. I've seen his mom's house and it's just a simple small-town home. It's nothing compared to this place, where one whole wall is made of glass windows that over-look the city of Houston.

His dad must really be a jerk for her to move away from all of this privilege and choose a small simple life instead. I guess that's why Liam doesn't want me to meet him.

"And here's my room," Liam says, finishing up the tour by saving his room for last. "It's a little better than my room at my mom's house."

I step inside and look around. This room is bigger than my mom's master bedroom. It's probably bigger than my dad's entire apartment. It has its own bathroom with a claw-foot tub and marble shower, and the walk-in closet is like a dream. One wall of his room is also open to the world below, made of glass.

"Aren't you scared people will see inside?" I ask. "With binoculars or something?"

He reaches over and flips a switch on the wall. A gray screen descends from the ceiling, slowly lowering over the windows until they're blocked off from the outside world.

"Nice," I say. I look around at his room décor, which his mostly dirt bike trophies and dark wood plaques that he's won in amateur racing series throughout his life. He has a king-sized bed with sheets so crisply tightened and tucked in that only skilled a maid could have pulled that off.

"Your life in Roca Springs is a lot different from your life here," I say.

He nods. "My life is, I guess. But I'm not. I'm still me," he says as he approaches me, sliding his hand down my arm. "All this wealth is my dad's, not mine."

"Didn't you just sign a contract?" I say, smiling to cover my extreme feeling of unworthiness. "You're kind of rich now, too."

His tongue slides over his lip while he watches me, those intense eyes pouring into mine. "Let's not talk about that stuff, okay? I'm in the bubble with you. I just really want to stay there."

I wrap my arms around him and rest my chin on his chest. "Okay," I say peering up at him. "Back into the bubble we go."

14

LIAM

I've spent my entire life training to become a professional motocross racer. I've been disciplined like an Olympian. I eat right, I work out, I stay away from alcohol or drugs that would ruin my health. I train, and train, and train. I work hard to get what I want.

But when it comes to love? I'm a total screw up.

I've flirted with a girl here or there, and even had a few sneaky make out sessions in the dark shadows of a motocross race. I've been on a date or two. None of it was serious. None of it mattered because as far as I was concerned, dating of all kinds would only ruin my motocross training.

I've screwed up badly with Bella. She's not just a summer fling. Not just a girl with a pretty smile and a great body. She's something more. Over these last few months, she's become the most important person in my life.

For the last eighteen years, I was the most important person in my life. I did everything for myself, to improve my life, and achieve my goals. Now, it's her. She's all I care about. I do still want my career, and Team Loco is an incredible opportunity that I can't pass up, but Bella is on my mind, all day every day. She consumes me. I don't want to leave her.

I know this is bad, but I don't care. In this moment, when she's standing here in the superhero shirt I bought her, with the lights of the city making her eyes shine while she stands in my bedroom, she's all I care about.

I lift her chin up to mine and kiss her softly. A soft sigh escapes her lips as her body melts against mine. It's been a long day of walking and exploring the comic convention, and now I just want to lay down. I circle my arms around her waist and lift her off the floor. She giggles, her lips pressed to mine, and I take a step backward until I sit on my bed, pulling her down with me.

"Whoa, this is a soft mattress," she says, sliding her hand down my comforter.

"Oh yeah," I say, falling back on the bed. I stare up at the ceiling and stretch out my limbs. "This bed is so much better than that crap I'm sleeping on at my mom's house."

Bella lays back, her head hitting the pillow next to mine. "I'm scared to ask how much this bed costs."

I laugh. "I don't even know. My dad bought it."

She turns on her side, facing me, and I turn to face her. "It's like when we Facetime," she says, grinning. "Only in person."

"Yeah, on Facetime, I can't do this—" I reach out and slide my arm around her hips and tug her close to me. Our bodies are just inches apart now. I bring my arm up her back and slide it through her hair.

Her lips slide into an easy smile, her eyes closing as she lays on my pillow.

I continue to caress her hair, my fingers trailing down her back and up her arm, and then to her cheek.

I lean in and kiss her. Her whole body awakens to my touch, and soon she's wiggling closer. Our legs tangle together and her breath hitches as our kisses deepen and grow more passionate. I pull away, leaving her breathless as I move to kiss her cheek, her neck, her collarbone. Her hands tangle in my hair, pulling me closer, always closer.

I know it'll only lead to pain, but I need this girl in my life.

Desire takes over, and my hand trails down to her hips, my finger sliding over that smooth skin just above her waistband.

My whole body floods with heat, passion, desire, as she holds the back of my head, kissing me with all that she has.

My hand slides up her side, reveling in the feel of her smooth skin. My thumb touches her bra. She freezes.

I open my eyes.

Bella's watching me, her expression like a deer in the headlights, "Maybe that's too much," she breathes, as she moves back an inch.

I move my hand. "Sorry."

She shakes her head. "No, it's okay… it's… fine."

But I can tell it's not fine.

"Bella, I'm sorry. We can stop."

She sits up and smoothes her shirt down. "I just don't know if we should do this—" She bites her lip, and the guilt on her face sends my heart tumbling. "It'll only end badly, you know?"

I nod. "It's okay, Bella. I promise. We can stop."

Her palm slides across her forehead and she groans. "Ugh, I feel like such an idiot."

"You are not an idiot," I say. I kiss her hand while it's pressed to her head.

"It's getting late. I should take you home."

She nods eagerly, and I smile and try to be lighthearted. I don't want her to think she's made me mad by stopping something before it went too far. She didn't. She's right, actually. We shouldn't have taken things any farther—not if we want to keep our hearts intact when this summer is over. Bella fidgets awkwardly on the elevator ride back down to the parking garage, so I start telling her a funny story of my childhood when I got stuck in these elevators. It makes her laugh. I know things are still weird, but at least they're better.

When we get to my truck, I pull open the door for her.

She stops and gives me a cute smile. "Aren't you the gentleman."

I shrug and return her grin, doing a silly little bow. "Only the best for my lady."

As we pull away from downtown, I can feel our metaphorical bubble stretching thin. It's easy to disappear into another city for the day and pretend that we're the happy couple we look like on the outside. But eventually, all bubbles pop, and ours is closer to that deadline than ever.

I look over at Bella while I drive. Not ten minutes on the highway, and she falls asleep, her head resting on the window. She looks so serene. Happy.

We have two weeks left of summer.

I don't know how I'll leave her when the time comes. But for now, the bubble is still there. There's still time to be with this girl who has captured every inch of my heart. And I'm going to stay here as long as I can.

15

BELLA

I wake up with a sharp pain in my neck. My eyes open slowly and I sit up, realizing I had been squished against the passenger door of Liam's truck. We're still on the road, but I recognize the area. We're just outside of Roca Springs.

I sit up straight and rub my neck. "Sorry. I guess I fell asleep."

Liam turns down the radio. "No worries. We're almost home, but I'm starving. Mind if I stop and grab something to eat?"

"I'm hungry, too," I say. "Let's stop at that diner."

"Even better," Liam says as he puts on his blinker and slows down. "I wasn't ready for our day to be over anyway."

It's no longer daytime. In fact, it's late at night, but I agree with him. I'm not ready for this one perfect day to be over. Tomorrow we go back to the real world, where superheroes don't exist and we're once again reminded that summer is almost over.

The diner is a classic truck stop place from the seventies and I don't think it's been remodeled since then. I've been here dozens of times with Kylie, and sometimes with my dad because he loves diner food. My mom prefers cleaner restaurants that don't smell like stale coffee and burnt eggs.

Liam and I slide into a booth at the far end of the restaurant, and we're clearly not the only teenagers who had the same late-night dinner plans. The place is packed with younger people, and a few older trucker guys. I don't recognize anyone from my school though, and no one recognizes us. It's a small blessing, and it means we get to stay in our bubble together while we eat dinner.

"I'm really sorry for freaking out earlier," I say as I pour a French vanilla creamer packet into my coffee.

"Seriously, Bella. No worries at all."

I look up at Liam. I trust him with my life, but I still feel so awkward about tonight. It could have gone far. It could have gone all the way. I know a huge part of me wanted that —wanted him. And maybe it would have been fun and maybe I could have moved on after summer and not had my heart destroyed. But I don't trust those maybes. I need to protect my heart, and keeping my clothes on is step one in the line of defense.

Our waitress defies the small-town diner stereotypes. Instead of some middle-aged woman with lots of makeup, who calls us "sweetheart", she's actually in her twenties. Her long brown hair flows loosely around her shoulders in a way that's probably not complying with local health codes. She's wearing jeans and a polo shirt with the diner's logo on it.

"What can I get for you guys?" she says with a heavy Texas accent. Okay, maybe that part fits the stereotype.

I order the blueberry pancakes with bacon and Liam orders the French toast with hash browns and bacon and a Dr. Pepper to go with his coffee.

"You needed a little caffeine to go with your caffeine?" I tease him.

He grins and flicks his wadded up straw wrapper at me. "Don't hate. I like coffee for before my food and soda for when I'm eating."

"So sophisticated," I say, tossing the straw wrapper back at him. "Your palate absolutely defines class and dignity."

"That's why you love me."

He's just playing around, but that word hits me straight in my core. Love.

I know I don't love Liam, not right now. It's too soon… we aren't official… I know all the reasons I don't love him.

But I *could* love this boy.

All it would take is the flip of a switch. The impossible becoming possible. In a different reality, where he wasn't some famous motocross racer but just a regular guy, I would love him. And maybe it's the mere thought of it that's making my heart race and my stomach feel all floaty.

Liam places the straw wrapper in his spoon and then flings it across the table at me. I hold up my hand to deflect it, but it lodges between my index and middle finger, making it look like I'm some kind of quick reflex ninja.

"Nice," he says.

The waitress brings our food, ending our war of the balled up straw wrapper. I don't know if I'm just super hungry, or if this place makes the best pancakes ever, but they're delicious. I try to eat slowly so I don't look like some gross slovenly eater in front of Liam, even though I tell myself it doesn't matter. I can look gross and slovenly right now. He's leaving soon, so why do I still want to impress him?

Being a woman is hard.

"Do we want to hit the track tomorrow?" Liam asks. Unlike me, he's already devoured most of his French toast in record time.

"Yeah sounds fun."

"I'll probably suck since I had to take an unplanned two weeks off," he says, grimacing.

I laugh. "Your version of sucking and my version of sucking are very different things. I'm sure you'll be great."

"I should really step up my training now that I'm on Team Loco. I have to prove my worth this season."

"You'll prove it," I say with full confidence. "They're lucky to have you."

He meets my eyes and we share a quiet moment that takes on a more serious tone. Even though motocross is what bonded us to each other, talking about it now feels more than awkward. There's a tension in the air when Team Loco is mentioned. How is it possible that this sponsorship is the greatest thing ever, yet also a dagger through the heart of our summer relationship?

"This is just my luck," I say, trying to make light of the situation. "I finally find a motocross guy who likes me and he goes off and gets famous and ruins it."

Liam shakes the hair from his eyes. He grins. "How do you think I feel? I met the girl of my dreams and now I have to leave her behind."

My whole body warms. I look down at my food, focusing on the one lone blueberry that rolled to the other side of the plate. "I doubt I'm actually the girl of your dreams…"

"How would you know? You haven't seen my dreams."

I roll my eyes, trying very hard to keep this lighthearted. "You're a charmer, you know that?"

His smile widens and I can see his shiny white teeth. "Only around you."

I take a deep breath and plunge my fork into a slice of my pancakes. I need to change the subject. This is too deep. Too real.

I glance over at the wadded up straw wrapper from before. "Whoa," I say, setting my fork down.

I pick it up and turn it over. "Is it just me, or does this look exactly like Squidward?"

"From Spongebob?" Liam says, his brows drawing together. He squints and then reaches for it. "Wow… it does." He examines it further. "It's uncanny."

I laugh and reach into my purse for my phone. "I need a picture of this or no one will believe it."

Liam sets it on the table for me to photograph. I unlock my phone and see a long list of notifications. Crap. When's the last time I checked my phone? I think it was back at Comicpalooza when we were taking photos with superheroes.

My smile fades as I see my mom and Brent's name on my phone screen. I've missed dozens of texts and calls from them.

"Uh oh…" I breathe.

"What's wrong?" Liam says.

I scroll through the messages, all of them asking where I am and why I haven't answered their calls. My phone was on silent and I didn't realize it. The last text from my brother says: *Mom is freaking out and wants to call the cops. Where the hell are you?*

"This is bad," I say. "My mom and brother are worried because they can't get ahold of me."

I check the time. "Oh god… it's past midnight. They've been trying to reach me for hours."

Liam curses under his breath. "Bella, I'm so sorry. I didn't even think about the time. Let's go, I'll get you home."

I text my mom and Brent back and tell them I'm fine and I'm almost home.

"It's okay," I say. "We can finish eating. They're already mad… what's an extra ten minutes going to do?"

Liam doesn't say anything but he doesn't look like he agrees with me.

Brent is the first to reply.

Brent: *Thank God you're okay.*

Me: *I'm fine. I just lost track of time. Sorry!*

Brent: *Tell that to Mom. She's pissed.*

I exhale and push my plate away. These pancakes might be amazing, but I'm not hungry anymore. I look up at Liam. "I think our bubble has officially popped."

16

LIAM

*B*ella's eyes have doubled in size. The blood has drained from her face as she sets her phone down.

"You okay?"

She shrugs and stares at her half-eaten food. "Brent said my mom is mad. I was having so much fun today I totally forgot to check in with them. And now I'm trying to think of how you're going to drop me off without them knowing I was with you since they're probably both watching the front window like hawks."

"It's okay," I say. "They know you're safe now. They'll calm down."

She shakes her head. "My mom, maybe. But not Brent. He's been waiting for me to screw up."

I take out enough cash to cover the bill and a tip and I leave it on the table. "Let's go," I say, reaching for her hand.

She takes it, and she holds my hand all the way back to my truck. I open the passenger door for her and she gets inside, finally releasing my hand. There's something final in the way she lets go of me, like she's already putting distance between us in her mind. The last time I held my truck door open for her we were joking around and having fun. This time the feeling in the air is exactly the opposite of fun.

I hate this. I wish Brent would just hear me out, forgive me, and trust me with his little sister. Things would be so much easier if not for the dark cloud of Brent Castro hanging over Bella's head. Sometimes I wonder what our relationship could be like if she wasn't always worried about getting in trouble with her brother.

The drive home is filled with nervous silence. I don't know what to say, so I keep my mouth shut. Bella fidgets with her seatbelt and her purse and her hair, unable to keep still.

"You should drop me off a few houses down," she says when I turn onto her street.

"No," I say. "That only makes you look guilty."

"Maybe I am guilty," she says, looking out the window.

"Guilty of what?" I say. "The only thing you did wrong was forget to check your phone."

She gives me a look. "You know it's more than that. I spent the day with you… if my brother finds out, I'll be dead."

"He doesn't get to control your life," I say as I pull into her driveway.

Bella looks so nervous she seems like she's about to crack apart into a million pieces. I reach over and cover her trembling hand with mine. "It's okay, babe. It'll all be okay."

Her front door swings open. Brent stands in the doorway wearing sweatpants and a tank top that reminds me exactly how huge he's gotten over the last year of bodybuilding. I'm not exactly a small guy, but I worry who would in a fight right now.

But I can't think like that. I won't fight Bella's brother, no matter how much he might hate me.

"Thanks for today," Bella says, throwing open her door. "I

really had a blast. Sorry it got ruined at the end." She jumps out of my truck and walks quickly her up driveway.

I leave the truck running, but I put the engine in park and I step outside.

Brent folds his arms across his chest and glares at me.

"Sorry I kept her out so late," I say. "We just lost track of time."

Bella spins around, eyes wide and terrified. "You should go," she whisper-yells.

"I thought I told you to stay away from my sister," Brent says, taking two steps closer to me. He's still far enough away to not be a threat, but I can see his muscles flex as he tightens his jaw and his hands clench into fists.

"Bella is old enough to make her own choices."

Brent sneers. "Sure she is. When the choice isn't you."

Bella rushes up to her brother and puts a hand on his chest. "Brent, just go inside. I'm home now. Drop it, okay?"

He ignores his sister's pleas, looking past her to glare at me. "Get off my lawn. If I see you again, I'll call the police."

I spin my truck keys around my finger. "I hate to break it to you, but the police can't do anything if no laws are being broken."

Maybe I shouldn't be sarcastic right now, but I can't help myself.

"I'll call you later," Bella tells me. Her eyes are pleading with me. "Please just go."

"She won't be calling you later," Brent says. "Your days of playing my sister are over."

"I'm not playing anyone." Now I'm pissed. I slam my truck door closed. "You need to get over your grudges and realize that Bella is an adult now. I've already apologized to you about the past. If you can't accept it and get over it, that's your problem. Not mine. And not Bella's."

I must have knocked all the words out of Brent because

he doesn't say anything over the next few seconds. Bella grabs his arm and tugs him toward the door. "Let's go," she says, her voice more authoritative than ever. Usually she's all sweet and placating when talking to her brother. Brent finally relents and he follows her inside. The door closes behind them and I'm left standing in her driveway, wondering if I'll ever get to come over here again.

Probably not.

I don't know why it was so important to me to get Brent's forgiveness and approval. It shouldn't matter. He hates me and he always will. After this summer, Bella will move on. I bet the next guy she dates will have a lot easier time winning over her brother's approval. He'd probably rather have her date a stick figure drawn on a piece of paper before me.

With a sigh, I turn back to my truck and I drive back home to my mom's house. Things really are different for guys than girls, because when I get back home just after midnight, no one is staying awake looking for me. I unlock the front door and slip inside quietly, making my way down to my temporary bedroom. This crappy little bed is going to be harder to sleep on tonight after I got a taste of my own bed today. It'll be even worse without Bella lying next to me.

Just before I close my eyes and go to sleep, my phone beeps.

Bella: *I'm really sorry for tonight.*

Me: *You don't have anything to apologize for.*

17

BELLA

"**W**hat is your *problem*?" I yell as soon as the front door closes behind us, putting a much needed solid wall between Brent and Liam. "This has nothing to do with you!"

Brent's nostrils flare. "It has everything to do with me when our mom calls me freaking out about you. We didn't know where you were or what you were doing."

"Mom knew I was at Comicpalooza," I say. "I was perfectly safe."

Mom's bedroom door creaks open down the hall. Brent and I turn to look at her. I brace for another verbal lashing, but Mom just looks at me through tired eyes. It's after midnight and she looks exhausted, her hair piled into a messy bun on top of her head. "I'm glad you're home safely," she says. Her gaze turns to Brent. "Son, you're making this worse than it is."

"How?" Brent says, throwing his arms up. "You're the one who called me in a panic because Bella wasn't answering her phone."

"That was earlier," Mom says softly. "Then we heard from

her, and she's fine. You really should calm down. All your yelling woke me up and I have work in the morning."

"Tell her she can't see him again," Brent says.

Mom lifts an eyebrow. "Who?"

"Liam Mosely. That's who she was with tonight. Tell her she can't see him."

Mom glances at me, and if I wasn't so angry at my brother, I might laugh at the expression she makes. "Seriously, Brent? You're acting like a child."

"Me?" Brent says, practically spitting the word. "I'm the only one here who actually cares about my sister's wellbeing."

"I trust Bella to make good choices in the company she keeps." Mom turns a pointed stare at Brent. "And you should too. Goodnight."

She disappears back into her bedroom, closing the door behind her. I know Brent still has a million things to yell at me about, but I'm not going to give him the chance. I run to my room – literally run – and quickly close the door. Sure, I'd like a shower, and maybe a snack since I barely ate my dinner, but I'm not risking it. I don't want to talk to my overbearing brother right now.

"This isn't over!" Brent calls out before he retreats to his own room.

I sit on my bed and glance at the wall that separates his bedroom from mine. When we were kids, it always brought me comfort to know that my brother was just on the other side of the wall. At Dad's apartment, we shared a bunk bed, and he was always just on the bunk below me. It used to be comforting to know my big brother was there, keeping me safe. A person I could run to no matter what happened, and he would be there for me. But times have changed.

He still sees me as a little kid he has to protect from the world. He refuses to believe that I could grow up, too, and that I could make my own choices and live my own life. Sometimes I wish he wouldn't come back from college at all.

I change into some pajamas and get into bed. I wish I could brush my teeth, but I absolutely refuse to go into the hallway before I know for sure that Brent is asleep. I'll wake up later on and do it. Right now, I'm avoiding him like the plague.

As soon as my head hits my pillow, I think about Liam. The day started out so wonderful, filled with new and exciting experiences and one ultra-romantic make out in his real bedroom. Then my brother had to ruin all of it. It's my fault, too. I should have checked my phone. I should have texted my mom and let her know I was okay. It's not like me to forget about my phone for hours at a time, but that's what happens when I'm around Liam. He makes me so happy, it's like the rest of the world doesn't exist. I guess that's what he meant about that metaphorical bubble he talks about. When we're in our bubble, it's just him and me and the rest of the world doesn't matter.

Now that bubble is officially gone, along with the last remaining days of summer.

I send him a text and his reply is almost immediate. I wonder if he was looking at his phone, thinking about me too?

Me: *I'm really sorry for tonight.*

Liam: *You don't have anything to apologize for.*

I want to keep the conversation going, but I know it'd be smarter to end it. Tonight's date is over. The summer is almost over. This summer fling is almost over.

Is this what all summer flings feel like? Like it's this perfect, happy thing that has an expiration date, but you can't just accept the date and move on. You have to hold onto it with all that you have, relishing in every moment, making memories that will seal themselves to your heart and never let you go.

Summer flings are supposed to be fun. That's how they're always talked about. Movies are made about them. Songs are sung about them. A fun, quick, summer fling. Instead it feels horrible. Like Liam and I are stuck in this desperate attempt to have as much fun as possible before the hands of time come and sweep it all away with the changing seasons.

I thought I knew how this would go. I thought I could have one of these so-called fun summer flings and then throw it all away at the end of summer. But I'm too attached. I like him too much. I've had too much fun. Too much happiness. Too many good memories. Liam is a part of me now. He's become so much more than just a silly fake boyfriend.

And now we have to break up and go on with our lives, and I'm supposed to act like it doesn't matter and like it's totally fine. Yeah, well, it's not fine. Not at all.

I WAKE UP THE NEXT MORNING FEELING EXACTLY AS AWFUL AS I did last night. Therefore, I decide to call in reinforcements. I've tried handling this heartache on my own all summer, but it just won't work. I show up at Kylie's house with a fresh batch of chocolate chip cookies and a tub of vanilla ice cream.

"You're lucky my brothers are at a friend's house today or they'd eat all of that before we got a chance," she says, laughing as she lets me into her house. "So what's up?"

All I did was text her half an hour ago saying I'm coming over. It was too much to say via text, but now that I'm here, it feels like too much to say in person, too. I gnaw on my lip and look around her empty living room. Kylie's parents are both elementary school teachers, so they're always home during the summer breaks.

"Are we alone?" I ask quietly.

"Yep," she says, heading into the kitchen. "My parents are visiting my Uncle Steve. They'll probably be there all day." She opens a cabinet. "Do we want bowls or should we just two-spoon it?"

"Two-spoon it," I say, setting the ice cream on her kitchen table and pulling off the lid. "This is an eat-straight-from-the-carton situation."

Kylie's brow furrows. "Uh oh."

She hands me a spoon and then reaches for a cookie. "Tell me all about it. What's up?"

I watch her while she scoops out ice cream and piles it on one cookie, then tops it with another cookie, making an ice cream sandwich. She hands it to me and then starts making one for herself.

I take a bite, trying to draw this out as long as possible. It's never fun admitting that you're a bad friend. Or a liar. And I've been both.

"Well?" Kylie says.

I sigh. "You know how you've sometimes been a bad friend?"

"Um, *rude*," Kylie says. "Did you bring ice cream and cookies just to insult me?"

I shake my head. "No. Sorry. I just... I want you to remember that you've sometimes been crappy too, that way you won't hate me when I tell you how crappy I've been."

Her eyes widen and she leans forward a bit. Ice cream melts from her cookie sandwich and she licks it off. "Details, Bella! What happened? What did you do? You brought ice cream and cookies so I'm thinking it was pretty bad..."

My teeth wear into my bottom lip. I know I just need to say it. Kylie is my best friend. She can handle that I've been lying to her… I think. But I can't stand the thought of her getting mad at me as much as my brother is. I can't deal with having both of them hate me right now.

I draw in a deep breath. "I've been lying to you all summer. About Liam."

I've been bracing for her to get mad at me, but her reaction is totally unexpected. Her lips slide into a wide grin, and her eyes sparkle mischievously. "Really?" she says, giving me a coy look that makes me feel dirty. "You two have been hooking up! I knew it!"

"No!" I say, sounding as scandalized as I feel. "We haven't *hooked up*!"

Kylie gives me a look that plainly says she doesn't believe me, and my cheeks burn hot with embarrassment.

I stare at my ice cream spoon. "Well… I guess it depends on your definition of hooking up."

Kylie gasps, putting a hand to her heart. "You kissed him! I *knew* it!" She takes a huge bite of her cookie sandwich and then leans forward, talking with her mouth full. "Tell me every detail. All of them. Leave nothing out. Is he a great kisser? Tell me all of it!"

I laugh. "I really thought you'd be mad about this."

"Why?" she says. "I don't have a crush on the guy… you do."

"Yeah, but I've been keeping it a secret. Actually, it's worse than that. I lied to you about it."

She shrugs off my concern. "It's fine, Bells. You're allowed to have secret crushes. You're not as open about that sort of thing as I am."

"I'm glad you're not mad, but I had to tell you about it today because—" Even after spending all morning rehearsing this talk in my mind, I'm still too embarrassed to say it out loud.

"What's wrong?" Kylie says. She straightens. "Did he hurt you?"

I shake my head. "Not intentionally… you see… it was more than just a one time thing. We had a fling."

Kylie doesn't look phased at all. "And?"

I swallow. "It was a summer fling. We agreed to it at the start of summer because we both liked each other… we said we'd have fun and secretly date and then we'd end things when summer was over."

"So he didn't do anything sleazy?" Kylie says. "I just want to make sure I don't need to go key his truck or something."

I laugh and shake my head. "No, he's been amazing. He even put up with Brent screaming at him last night."

"So what's the problem?" she says. "If you feel bad that you kept it from me, don't. It's fine, Bella. I am glad you told me now though so we can gush about him. You still haven't told me if he's a good kisser."

"He's a great kisser," I say. "But the problem is… well…" I look up at my best friend and lay out my feelings more honestly than I ever have before. "I got too attached. I don't want to let him go, but I have to. We agreed on it. Summer is over soon and we'll be over too."

Tears flood into my eyes and I blink them away. Kylie stands up and walks over to me, her short black hair tickling my face as she squeezes me into a bear hug. "I'm sorry, Bells."

She pulls away after a moment and kneels down so that she's eye level with me. "You know what you need to do, right?"

I shake my head. A single tear rolls down my cheek.

Kylie takes both of my hands in hers. "You gotta rip off the band-aid."

"Huh?"

She gives me a sad grin. "Remember when we were in seventh grade I fell on the concrete during lunch and skinned up my knee real bad? The nurse put that huge bandage on it and I went home and my mom told me I had to take it off and clean the wound but I didn't want to because it was going to hurt so bad. Remember that?"

I nod, the memory resurfacing clearly in my mind. "I made you rip it off."

"Yep. You told me to just rip it off fast and easy so that it wouldn't hurt as much."

"And that's what I need to do with Liam," I say, digging my spoon into the ice cream. I take a huge bite and the sudden cold makes my head hurt.

"You're right," I say after the pain wears away and I'm reaching for another bite of sweet, cold, sugary heartbreak-healing ice cream. "This summer fling is the bandage on my heart. I just need to rip it off and not drag it out."

"Yep," Kylie says, standing up and reaching for another cookie. "Trust me. It's the best way."

LIAM

I'm making a turkey and cheddar sandwich when someone knocks on the door. My mom does a lot of online shopping, so deliveries are dropped off nearly every day. I ignore the knock, assuming it's just another package for her.

Then I hear my mom swing open the door and say, "Well hi there! How are you, sweetheart?"

She only calls one non-family member by the name *sweetheart*. I set my knife down on top of my half-made sandwich and peek around the kitchen cabinets.

Bella is here.

"Liam, you have a guest," Mom says as she sweeps past me. "Offer her a sandwich, okay?"

"That's okay, I'm not hungry," Bella says. She smiles at me, but it's broken. I guess she still feels awkward after last night.

"Hey," I say, giving her a quick hug. "You sure you don't want a sandwich? My sandwich making skills are perfectly average. You won't be disappointed, nor will you be overwhelmed."

Her broken smile heals a bit and she shakes her head.

"No, thanks. But I'll hang out with you while you eat."

"It won't take long," I say as I go back to assembling my sandwich.

"Oh I know," she says, taking a seat at the kitchen table. "You're the fastest eater I've ever seen."

"I'm a growing man," I say playfully.

The conversation stays light because we both know my mom and Phil are in the other room and could be over-hearing everything we say. I chomp down on my food and finish it in just a couple of minutes.

"What's up?" I say as I shove a handful of chips in my mouth. "Wanna go ride today?"

She shakes her head. "Nah. I'm not really in the mood right now."

To anyone else, that might sound like a regular thing to say. But I know it's not normal for Bella. She loves motocross. She loves the track. It's how we met each other, after all. It's how we spent most of our time together this summer.

"You want to take a walk?" I ask.

She nods. "Sure."

My mom and Phil's house sits on several acres of land, and my mom has made herself quite an impressive garden in the back yard. Gardening has become her favorite hobby since moving away from the big city and settling down here in the country. Our backyard has vegetables, fruits, and so many flowers you'd think we're actually a plant store instead of a private home.

Bella and I wander through the garden path, which is made of concrete stepping stones and gravel. I want to hold her hand, but the seriously strained vibes rolling off her tell me I probably shouldn't.

"Are you okay?" I ask.

She shrugs. "No."

"What happened after I left last night?"

"Not much," she says, shoving her hands in her pockets while we walk. "I just went to bed. Brent was gone when I woke up this morning."

"Was your mom mad?"

"Surprisingly not." Bella reaches for a pink rose and brings it closer to her face so she can smell it.

"Bella, what's on your mind?"

She freezes, and my question hangs in the air for a long, uncomfortable moment. I shift on my feet. "It's not like you to come over without texting me first. So what's going on?"

She looks up at me with tears in her eyes. "Dang it," she says, blinking. "I told myself I wasn't allowed to cry."

My heart seizes up in my chest. "Why would you cry? Bella, what's wrong?"

She shakes her head, more as a response to herself than to me. "You know what's wrong," she says. "This has to end."

"This?"

"Us," she says, holding her chin high. Her bottom lip trembles but she looks me right in the eyes as if she has more confidence than she really does. "We have to end this summer fling. The summer is over, so we're over."

"The summer is not over," I say in a rush. It feels like my whole body is on fire. It feels like I should run away from this whole conversation because I refuse to believe it's happening. "It's not over. We still have time."

"Like what, a week and a half?" she says, rolling her eyes. "That's not time. That's a slow, painful breakup. We should just end things quickly right now. Just—" She snaps her fingers. "Just end it. We can even lie to each other and say we'll stay friends."

"That's not a lie. I'll always be your friend."

She lets out a sarcastic snort of laughter and turns away from me, running her fingers along a flowerbed of daises. "As nice as the sentiment is, we won't be friends, Liam. You'll be famous and I'll be some small town nobody."

"You're not a nobody." I grab her arm and turn her around to look at me. "You're my girlfriend."

"I'm your summer fling."

"You call it what you want and I'll call it what I want."

Her lips press into a thin line like she's trying really hard to be mad at me. But I know Bella. She's not mad. She's hurt.

"Babe…"

"Don't *babe* me," she says, her voice trembling. "I'm not your babe."

"Bella." I cup my hand on her cheek, wiping away her tears with my thumb. "We can call it whatever we want, but you and I both know that what we have is more than just some stupid fling. It's real. Or at least it feels like it to me. I thought you felt it, too."

She looks down at our feet, and her shoulders sag. "I don't know what it feels like to me," she says softly. "Just that it feels like heartbreak."

"I don't want you to hurt." I wrap my arms around her and kiss the top of her head. "Bella, that's the last thing I want."

"It's not your fault. I knew what I was getting into." She peers up at me and all I want in this world is to kiss her one more time. "This has to end," she says. "We're already hurting. Why should we drag it out more?"

Deep down, I think I know she's right. But it's taking everything I have not to argue. I want to drop to my knees and beg and plead with her to change her mind. I just need another week. Another day. Another hour with this girl.

Bella holds her head high and takes a step backward, putting just a few inches between us but god, it feels like miles. "I think it's better this way."

I nod, and now hot tears are pooling in the corners of my

eyes. I can't remember the last time I cried—maybe at my grandmother's funeral ten years ago. Maybe a little bit that time I dislocated my shoulder and it hurt worse than any injury I'd ever had. But I've definitely never cried over a girl.

"I'm so sorry," Bella says. "It was fun while it lasted, and you're seriously a great guy. But it has to be over now."

The lump in my throat is threatening to suffocate me. "Okay," I manage to say, even though all the air feels like it's been drop-kicked out of my lungs.

"We can break up now," I say. "But please stay my friend. I don't think I could handle it if you start hating me."

She nods softly as a gentle summer breeze carries the fragrance of the flowers all around us. "We'll always be friends."

"Always." I swear I'm about to break into a million pieces. How is Bella holding herself together so well? I'm two seconds away from being completely destroyed.

"Good luck on Team Loco," she says. At some point in this conversation, we turned back toward the front yard, and we're almost back to her truck. "I'll be rooting for you."

"Thanks. I get free tickets, so maybe you could come to the Houston race."

"That would be fun." She takes her keys out of her pocket and stands near her truck.

"Text me any time," I say, just because I don't want this conversation to end.

"Sure," she says, opening her door. "You too."

And then she starts the engine and backs out of my driveway. I stand here, watching her drive away until her taillights are just tiny imperceptible dots on the horizon. And I know what we were—just summer flings. I know that this is what we agreed on. I know it has to be over now.

But I also know one more thing.

I'll do whatever it takes to get her back.

Thank you for reading Bella and the Summer Fling!

Bella and Liam's story continues in Book 3, Bella and the One Who Got Away.

IT WAS SUPPOSED TO BE A SUMMER FLING. I ENDED THINGS with Liam the moment summer was over, just as we agreed. I moved on with my life. Easy peasy.

Well, that's what I'm trying to do. College classes are boring, and I there's nothing to do in my small town. Everything reminds me of Liam. He's everywhere lately now that he's a famous motocross racer. I see him on TV, online, and printed on T-shirts. He's every fangirl's crush, but he was my crush first.

And now he's gone.

ABOUT THE AUTHOR

Amy Sparling is the bestselling author of books for teens and the teens at heart. She lives on the coast of Texas with her family, her spoiled rotten pets, and a huge pile of books. She graduated with a degree in English and has worked at a bookstore, coffee shop, and a fashion boutique. Her fashion skills aren't the best, but luckily she turned her love of coffee and books into a writing career that means she can work in her pajamas. Her favorite things are coffee, book boyfriends, and Netflix binges.

She's always loved reading books from R. L. Stine's Fear Street series, to The Baby Sitter's Club series by Ann, Martin, and of course, Twilight. She started writing her own books in 2010 and now publishes several books a year. Amy loves getting messages from her readers and responds to every single one! Connect with her on one of the links below.

www.ingramcontent.com/pod-product-compliance
Lightning Source LLC
Chambersburg PA
CBHW022143150726
47992CB00002B/729